Better Placed Elsewhere

THE LIVING WITH THE PAST ANTHOLOGY

By Mark Rayner

FIRST EDITION:

Better Placed Elsewhere

THE LIVING WITH THE PAST ANTHOLOGY

By Mark Rayner

"It's not for us I'm afraid!"

various:

FOR THE VERY FIRST TIME, FRESH FROM THE ISLE OF WIGHT, MARK BRINGS YOU A COLLECTION OF STORIES THAT SIMPLY WEREN'T CONSIDERED GOOD ENOUGH – FROM THE SLUSH PILES SENT TOPPLING ACROSS THE WORLD...

MARK HAS COLLECTED TOGETHER THE UNSUNG HERO'S OF HIS ARCHIVES – THE ONE'S THAT MIGHT HAVE MADE IT; NEARLY MADE IT AND COULD HAVE MADE IT...

THE STORY TOO COMPLEX FOR INTERZONE; THE CLASSIC HE WAS INSPIRED TO WRITE WHILE A RAT WAS CHEWINGTHROUGH HIS BOILER CABLE AT HOME AND A HOST OF RE-WORKED LAST DITCH INTERNET FRIENDLY SAGAS...FINALLY PLACED IN A NICE BOOK THAT TAKES UP LESS SPACE THAN A HARD-DRIVE..STORIES THAT WERE CONSIDERED: BETTER PLACED ELSEWHERE!

First Published in Great Britain in November 2013 by Kindle Direct Publishing

CONTENTS:

ACKNOWLEDGEMENTS

I need here to take a moment to thank lots of people; let's hope that I don't miss anyone out...

Firstly, to Justin and Paul they are both responsible for helping me salvage the files that held the slightly more pompous sounding version of this book 'LIVING WITH THE PAST' and giving me the chance to restore the lost files; Paul is also responsible for reminding me that occasionally it's fine to write material that might shock your mother – hopefully not so much in this volume.

My Sister Lynne, whose comments and line by line dissections of my earlier works remarked upon it's grim reality. A writer needs a market so it's time for a nod of thanks to Michael Whitewood and his fanzine "Yoko Scrum"

Two of the tales in this collection were previously inspired by my nephew Ben, who inspired the story of "CAMPING TRIP" and "THE LITTLE BOY IN THE MIRROR" and my late Uncle David who was always encouraging and provided the inspiration for the story "DO YOU REMEMBER ME?"And, not forgetting Redge, Smudge and Digby. Oh yes just time to mention my Pen Pal Wayne, Faith, Faye, Jemma, Mel, Lyn, Lynne, Nicki , Ziggy, Jenna, Jane, Robert , Mike, Jacky, Libby, H and Sam X2.

I'll thank Jo Drake, formerly of Solent Tv for all around support when I began work and also for providing the title – as Jo will notice, one story I have always intended to include has been especially re-edited for this volume.

Finally, a big thank you to Channel Four and Chat Magazine and all my friends at a certain DIY STORE on the Isle of Wight that likes the colour orange.

FOREWORD BY MARK RAYNER

It's October 15th 1996 and it's just gone 5.35pm – and it's dark. I'm standing outside the BBC TELEVISION CENTRE attached to a microphone and I'm wearing my Dad's favourite green coat.

In two days time, Channel Four are going to transmit my report to the nation and I'll be getting an audience of just over 5 million people opposite Noel's House Party – and then I'll disappear back into obscurity – my next time on telly will gain the lowest audience of the 21st Century when the transmitter is struck by lightning..

Funny old thing hindsight; it's a little over a year since I joined a Correspondence Writing Course and on this cool October night, well I'm on a natural high - all my writing projects have what publicity departments call a 'hook' , a tag, a saleability factor and on Saturday the 17th I'm going to go head to head with Noel Edmonds and discuss the censorship of Australian soaps; that will begin a book idea – an A-Z and by the start of the new millennium that will be lost on a hard-drive; like some of the best novels ever written – and they say everyone has a novel in them or so it's been said; back in 1996 I have two -
'TIMEBURN' a trilogy that doubtless still wakes my tutor in a cold sweat; and 'EQUILIBRIUM' –a Doctor Who proposal for the Paul Mcgann era novels – this was eventually rejected by BBC BOOKS in 1998; and by then they'll be a sitcom – yes a sitcom – when I finally get a new word processor the first task will be sending out the rewritten script with mere weeks to go for BBC TALENT – it didn't win, it was in the running for SKY DIGITAL PRODUCTION, long story - and back here in 1996 all these ideas are forming; along with a collection of short stories – my 'LIVING WITH THE PAST' anthology; this begins with a work for radio...

A freelance writing career can cover many different mediums and take your work all over the world and my story begins at Radio Four - it's time for Fifteen Minute Theatre...

Radio is such an amazing market for a writer- it gives such a limitless market for your ideas and radio stations back then were 'crying out' for material and it's true most coffee break fiction of the time translated well to the fifteen minute format – in fact, to train myself to write good short fiction we'd been advised to read our stories onto audiotape – it helps to get the feel for the drama and the dialogue of the story. I'd written a few plays in my time, little plays for stage and audio dramas including the topical 'CHRISTMAS SKYDROP' and some unperformed triumphs back in the mid-eighties, and I'd listened to radio for years.

I finally settled down to write Family Tree in December 1999; this little tale was going to be perfect – I could even hear the voice of Maurice Denham reading it out as I wrote. FAMILY TREE came in two versions – an audioplay with cast narration and the fifteen minute narrative.

My tutor couldn't begin to understand how the sound of someone completing a jigsaw could be accomplished on radio, although he thought it was an excellent story – Radio Four did too, they wanted me to send it back in 6 months for reconsideration.

Six months later it went back – I was really enthusiastic because they'd asked me to send it back when they had some gaps. So, I settled back and waited; with radio you always get a reply and a reason for the rejection – so I was told, well the slots were oversubscribed and I found the radio market to be distinctly lacking in any requirement for my work, I'm afraid 15 minute theatre went the same way as 'Right to Reply' – without any comment whatsoever..

It wasn't a total loss however it was excellent training for writing short stories and learning what works in fiction and there was another plus – the story was also suitable for some obscure and online US titles that were crying out for short fiction - and remains a strong possible for an audio version of this anthology.

Here is a slightly polished version of that story, I hope you enjoy it...

INTRODUCTION

Hello Everyone and a warm welcome to my first anthology and I know what you're thinking this is the point where that person you've never heard of lets his ego expand to fill the word count...

Not guilty your honour – it's true I've published this anthology: but why?

Well, writers, especially when they're just starting out and learning their craft tend to build up quite a portfolio of rejected work; the comments I've received more often than not "We quite enjoyed reading this, but this isn't quite right for our coffee break/ Twist of the knife/ fiction page – so, you make a few changes, some subtle alterations and you post it on..and on.. and then you realise two things – one that the original is still the best – and two – that the market is - despite the many internet forums and competitions still not that large and still mostly closed until you start to find other avenues for your work; Science Fiction titles and sitcom competitions and then you see that the market is massive! It's just limited to your style of fiction...

Oh, and the only thing that stops you from getting published is the cost of posting; the availability of time; the 'style' of your work; the length of your stories - and the realisation that times have moved on – it's now cheaper to go through the files select some gems and publish a book, my rejected works' you might say... Or that was the plan – in 2007 my computer died – luckily, I always save to hard-copy and to floppy – I took the decision to stop sending any-more stories out, although the comments were still pretty good and I had planned to get interest in a couple of novels I'd been working on – I initially took the crash of my hard-drive as nature's way of telling me to take a year out: but I was invigorated by my 'gap' year and when the floppy files were salvaged onto disc – I knew that now was time.

Please join me as I share the story of my stories, the good, the not very good and the unpublishable and you never know you might just enjoy the journey...

Family Tree

Nobody knew what had happened to Albert.

It was a mystery, unsolved; there was speculation of course, over many years; his brother, Archie had his own theories too, but he never, once spoke of them to his mother. He had promised her on her deathbed that he would let the matter rest and not let it ruin his life as it had hers. Then, one morning as he switched on the radio, Archie had no way of knowing that answers would arrive at his doorstep: Whether, he wanted them or not.

'A skeleton believed to be that of a young child has been found during building work for Fine Oak Housing Estate in Essex, the matter is being investigated. There are no further details at present.'

Archie slumped into his chair in shock. He glanced accusingly at the radio, unable to comprehend what he was hearing. The gentle tick of the clock on his sideboard was sending him gently back...

The cracking sound of the broken bark as you lashed out at each other before making your way through a warm sunny September afternoon. They were playing at being Pirates and they had no conception of time. As it got darker, they would run home only stopping to check on their hideout, a sheltered area of the wood, with spiteful bean cans rusting out of sight; they always seemed delayed there until the last whispers of the evening.

'There you are, I have been going out of my mind so I have!' Mother, would be waiting to bark at them on their return.

Yet, her mood would soon lighten and she would clasp them to her bulging chest and Archie remembered her in a dark blue pinafore with yellow flowers, silly really.

It was strange how the nights when they lost track of time were always bath nights and the water was always warmest when at its muddiest.

Archie recalled how his knees singed to the side, he was never burnt Mother would pop her weathered nose around the door and bring in some towels. Concerned that they would perish from some vile infection her drying technique was never cruel and patiently dignified, and Archie could now bathe in the memory...

The news report continued to plague Archie all that morning until he practically fell over a fellow resident, while rushing to switch on the television for the lunchtime bulletin. This, turned out to be a visual repeat of the radio broadcast with a camera close-up of a new housing estate and several workers crowded around a muddy digger.

The reporter at least sounded more caring and his tone was warm.

'I have to make a phone call,' Archie attracted Faye's attention. Faye was an assistant who had came to the home a year or two back on a Government Training Scheme. She always helped Archie with tasks made painful by his arthritis.

'-Certainly, Mr Cartwright. 'These days, phones were common place, back then a ringing phone *terrified* him; It had its own special place, had to, because of the size of the things. You treated it with pride, like old soldiers, you respected them, yet you quaked in their presence.

'Mr Cartwright,' Archie found himself being pulled back from the cloakroom of memory. Faye was smiling sweetly and patiently her brown hair was in a perfect bun and good heavens, was that a nose stud? Still, each to their own , long as she had a good love life.

'Oh, I'm sorry, my dear, the local police. I have some information...'. He sounded most insecure. 'I have some information about a case...'. Archie smiled.

For a moment, he could see Albert stood beside him, bare knees and worn green shorts, an indignity pacified by the blazer, which was as impracticable as ever.

4

He preferred to remember his brother carefree and tatty; Not the authoritarian substitute of those sepia prints.

'Your brother disappeared in that area?'

Archie nodded, meeting the eyes of the Police Sergeant. Good of the officer to take them to his private office, especially when there was such a flap on. The Sergeant placed a pudgy finger on the map he had gleaned from an old AA guide.

'Well, that seems to fit with the location...'

Archie nodded again. He could tell he was satisfied they found their man, eh, boy. Faye was smiling back at him with concern. She was there for moral support as well as transportation.

'They were beautiful woods back then,' Archie recalled. 'I gather they're a housing estate now?' He hadn't meant to sound quite so snobbish, especially when the Sergeant pointed out that his daughter lived there, well near there.

Fortunately, Faye lightened the mood when her mobile went off. Some business with Mrs Leonard's medication and she warned her understudy that she ate them like "Smarties.".At that point the Officer called for tea all round and asked Archie if he were staying with anyone: A most curious question.

'Why? Are you offering me a room Sergeant?'

The Sergeant laughed it off good-naturedly. Faye explained that she would keep an eye on him as always and Archie wished she had not. Archie, had no intention of doing himself in, that Ethel Skinner had a lot to answer for; It was the most appalling cliché that the elderly sat at home brandishing their razor blades and painkillers at the slightest trauma.

'You don't have to worry about me Sergeant...' Archie explained gently. 'I just need to know. You understand?' If Sergeant Bailey did not then Archie figured he never would, yet in that twinkle in his eye Archie could see that he did.

'Thank you for your time Sir, we shall try our best to investigate further...'

Faye took that as the cue to leave and Archie followed, noting the gentle request by the speed that Bailey guided them towards the door. He knew Albert was dead. He had always felt it.

Although she had her orders to get Archie back as soon as possible, Faye could not help the temptation to visit the building site where they had discovered the skeleton. Archie had to see, Faye knew how important it was to him. He might have spent those moments wandering the fields of his past - but fortunately, the site forewoman, a young Irish woman named Kelly, was most sympathetic - after Faye explained about the skeleton, Kelly arranged a hard hat recky of the location.

Everyone was worried about Archie that evening. If truth be told, he had a lot to think about. Archie made some excuse about wanting to finish his book, or that impossible flowery jigsaw that Faye had bought him for Christmas. Either way, the light was poor and Albert was in his thoughts tonight.

'Make sure you put your coat on, you little devil,' his mother had said that last day. The day seemed to last forever in his memory.
Archie had blundered around calling Albert's name, as he still did every wet Wednesday or whenever his mind had wandered over the thresholds of his realisation. He could still hear the trees in the forest screaming out their silence.
There was never a trace: Until now .Archie knew it, just knew it. Albert had died in those woods.

At Christmas after Albert 'left' they had a toast to absent friends. Yet, Albert had always been there, even at Archie's wedding to Sylvia Albert was mooching in the background side stepped but patient, as if awaiting that last dance.
'Mr Cartwright you have a visitor,' Faye's voice chipped away at his grey memories . 'Mr Cartwright, there's someone to see you. Shall I tell him to come back tomorrow?'
Archie hurried, always pleased to have guests. Fortunately this visitor was in deep conversation with Faye in the hallway.

'Hello.' Archie poked his nose outside.

'Good evening. I heard about the discovery in the woods, I thought you might like some company.' The visitor was a small black bearded man in a blue striped suit. Archie raised an eyebrow as the man produced a bottle.

'Jolly decent of you, have we met?'

'Terrance,' they shook hands and Archie noted how sweaty Terrance's palms were. 'I know it has been a long time.' Terrance apologised, noting how Archie had begun to gape at him.

'No, do please sit down.' Archie showed the man in and tried to place him in his memory.

Terrance picked up a piece of the jigsaw and instantly slotted it into position. 'Takes a while for all the pieces to fit...' Archie muttered to himself...

'I am sorry I didn't make the wedding.' The visitor placed his bottle on the old man's sideboard.

'That was over thirty years ago!'

'Closer to forty!' Terrance calculated.

'Really?' Archie was feeling older than ever now, in the time since he had last met Terrance his dear wife had died and his mother too.

'Well yes, I suppose it must be...'

Terrance had perched himself on the unmade bed. An odd little man he was too like an elderly elf, a little goblin that was it, there was something about him that made Archie, wonder, that was it.

'I stayed in touch as long as I could. Father, moved away.' The visitor recalled his eyes like dewdrops.

'It must be hell for you at the moment, having your family history dredged up.'

Yet, Archie had to disagree, when you had lived as long as he had you tended to let those in your "family" to drift a little from your thoughts. It seemed only fair that they had an airing.

'There's little history, besides the bones, cross-contamination the technical boys call it...' Archie glowered. This report, meaning the numbskulls had driven over the bones before they realised what they had.

'I will get some wine glasses...' Archie smiled. He wanted to get

7

out of the room because Terrance looked uneasy.

'No, don't!' Terrance tried to hold him back. 'I only really came to give you this...'. He searched briefly in his jacket and produced a dusty green cap.

'I really do not touch the stuff!' Terrance eyed the bottle nervously.

'Are you all right?' Archie intricately studied the cap.

'Someone just walked over my grave...'; The visitor admitted, spluttering as he patted Archie's shoulder.

'I was a little older than you, when your brother died, older but not much wiser.' Archie had blown hat dust in Terrance's direction and Terrance fixed his gaze right on him. 'I thought, as long as I had that, it was like holding Albert's heart.'

'If the police had this, it might have led them to his real killer,'

'I know there were a lot of rumours, speculation. Even my own father was suspected.'

'Is, that why you left?' Archie reasoned.

Terrance nodded. 'What I mean to say is...,' Terrance rubbed his nose with a handkerchief. 'You mustn't assume that Albert was murdered. It really wasn't like that...'.

'I don't understand...' Archie gasped. 'You know how Albert died? How do you know how Albert died? They never found his body!'

Terrance breathed in. 'I, found his body...' He stopped. 'It wasn't difficult. I saw him fall. 'The curious little man was speaking so emotively, yet so softly that Archie might have missed what he was saying completely. Archie could hear Mrs Leonard's antique clock very clearly through the partition wall. Archie could always hear it when he was concentrating and now it sounded louder than ever.

Tick

Tick.

Tick

'One moment he was laughing at the top of the tree, then, he wasn't.' Terrance's voice-raised tempo, as he thought for a moment that Archie would smash the bottle down on his head.'I panicked, buried the body.'

For a moment, Archie thought he could see the weights as they

8

lifted from an old chum's shoulders. In the corner of the room, Albert was smiling as if he were a mediator in a very bitter moment.

'What's to celebrate?' Archie placed the bottle gently down. He glared, Archie had always been fussy about who he drank with. 'You never told my mother or confessed to anyone?' The rage was soaking through him.

'I tried to, but she was old before her time, she didn't take it in and how could I prove it was an accident?' Terrance looked up despairingly. Archie grunted and flung the cap across the room. 'I thought they would send me to the gallows and it was only an accident.'

'So your conscience was clear?' Archie studied the visitor's face for any sign of one.

'It weighed on my mind for many years, and I even called our first son "Albert".'

'Poor little, sod!' Whispered Archie.

'I was always thinking why?' Terrance blinked away his tears and now he was sobbing all over Archie's carpet.

'Oh, "Why?" Archie glared at him. 'I know "Why?"! I have a last day etched in my mind's eye - but it's a fake.'

'What?' Terrance gaped. So Archie explained. The last day was a fake because he was tucked up in bed with a nasty cold. The intervening years had dulled the image, because the day before Albert vanished, someone now very close threw a bucket of water over Archie, one Terrace Oliver that was who.

'I'm sorry!' Terrance backed off.

'So when I couldn't sleep, I thought "Why?" My mother, she wondered "Why?" She slapped me around the face when I said Albert wasn't safe in the forest.' His face still stung at the thought of it.Archie allowed the moment to simmer through him, it was if for the first time in many decades... He realised it was not his fault.

'I expect you'll have to call the police?' Terrance spoke resignedly.

Archie frowned. Just what would he tell them? That Terrance had found a body and buried it? They had wanted to do that themselves; Give themselves a sense of completion.

'We wanted to put the matter behind us, where it must be you

9

see?'

Terrance could scarcely believe his good fortune, even after Archie explained that he would not expose his part in all this. 'So, you're not going to expose me?' He stared.

'I don't have to, I have my answers and if the Police are that bothered they will track you down...' Archie thought on and added sourly. 'If that happened, I would have, to tell them, what you told me.' No other way, Archie realised, unless he knowingly withheld information from the police.

Terrance took one last glance towards the bottle of wine as he headed towards the door. 'Oh, you won't tell the police, I guarantee it.'

So the old man was getting cocky and confident now that Archie had let him off the hook. Sad. Archie had expected noble gratitude - still, it must be tough when you had kiddies to worry about.

At that moment, Faye's voice came through the door. She was asking Archie if his brother was still with him? It was getting late and would Albert like to stay for dinner?'

Archie looked at the bottle of cherry wine and saw red. He was raging at Terrance, with every ounce of hatred from the last sixty years. 'You were never going to confess! The only reason you came here was because they uncovered your handiwork. The only person you told was my ailing mother, and you haven't even got the decency to use your real name!' Archie reasoned he should have done this a long time past, stand up to this bully.

Terrance was a coward. No-one would discover the truth because of him. Because of him, Albert was to be consigned to the history books, as just a lot of old bones and the last rants of a silly old man. He had bought wine and biscuits to butter him up? Archie picked up the bottle and lunged determinedly towards his guest.

'You think they're going to say "Poor old duffer, got a bit confused." Then just fade away?'

Then there was the sound of breaking glass...

The news at One was read that day, by a bemused young woman who could scarcely believe her luck and this showed in her voice.

'A man has appeared in court charged with the attempted murder of his friend Terrance Oliver, although the accused hit Mr Oliver over the head with a bottle, the case does have a most bizarre twist...'; And it did. The wine bottle had been laced with a substance which would almost certainly have killed Archie had he indulged. Terrance had planned to cleanse his own conscience by confessing to the one person who would never expose him

One final mystery remained: Archie could not fathom - how Terrance had managed to bury the body, and how it had stayed hidden for so long? Perhaps the tale of a little boy lost in the forest had scared others from looking too closely: Perhaps not.

Maybe it was fate.

Or maybe someone else had lent a hand.

FINDING A WRITING STYLE:

My first short stories were appalling! I just couldn't get them right –
but with some research - and some special Fiction publications I was
soon able to have my stories unleashed on a wider audience – they
were still rejected but the comments improved, these early tales
break all the rules; there are cardboard characters; prostitution and
murder – enjoy!

Short Circuit

'One day I'm going to trade in that old thing!'
Brian was speaking to mother on the phone as I, struggled to decipher the worn text beneath the aged typing ribbon.

'Pardon?' I glared up from my manuscript, knowing that he meant the typewriter: but why did he consider my possessions to belong to him?

This was my typewriter; Old unreliable and no longer in the peak of condition - like a lot of things, I know.

Anyway it makes me angry: I get very defensive when he talks of trading it in; me? I'd prefer to bury it in the back garden - like snuffles, we've been through a lot. When I look back, it is a wonder I ever learnt to read at all: The kids had started nursery school before I finally did something about it; Anyway, I enjoy it: The flow of words, the tune of sentences: Brian's always been the one to keep me grounded in a reality of sorts; When he made the decision to replace old faithful, he may as well have been stepping on my dreams: I'm building up to a word processor!

'I don't want a computer!' I insisted, 'wouldn't mind an office though...'.Typing at the kitchen table is not my ideal! You know what they say about writing at the table? There's always a washing basket! ; A dishwasher to empty a radio to hear the news on: A soap to psychoanalyse! Distractions at the door never came until I set up shop on the kitchen table.

So, next day when Brian arrives back with a big grin I hadn't seen since that first night of our honeymoon....

I didn't even have to look, I knew and the kids were also in on the 'surprise'.

'I promise you dear. It's not another cat!' He determinedly opened the boot.

So, there it sits: I feel so guilty like an old friend's caught me with a cheeky new lover: My new 'Personal Computer' honestly, I could have retched!

'I can even use it for doing the books' Brian's bald-spot shines all the lighter, as if this off the cuff comment wasn't scrawled first on his hand.

My son's comment that it had great educational use doesn't over-enthuse me either: Strange how kids flock to education when they need a viable excuse for wasting their lives: It would be like my son asking me for advice on how to snog a girl at the fifth form disco that he should ever seek educational solace: Never happen... And Internet ready? Well it would be, wouldn't it? I knew what was coming, although I had to admit it was a good buy! Goodbye to my writing career!

'I'm just reading the Buffy homepage...' My son, Justin protests.

'I won't be a moment love. The printer's the problem!' Brain never read the manual - it's a wonder we have two kids! Maybe, I wouldn't have minded so much but things escalated from there; my daughter could chat to a boy in Hong Kong, whereas I'd begin by chasing a cursor, typing great wads in, pushing letters from left to right; Sometimes, left watching as my beloved musings crashed into Neverware...In time, I became a kitchen refugee, having to entertain total strangers while my daughter's popularity sky-rocketed.

Luckily, I was not the only one lacking in computer know-how: They set up a ghetto for us poor uninitiated and even got government financing for basic courses at my lifeline, the local college.

'What I really need help with, is extracting my offspring from it!' I joked with my tutor.

'Yes, that can be a problem!' My tutor laughed with me in a manner suggesting a fellow sufferer.

Later, that evening: I put my foot down. 'This is not a toy. It's for my writing!' I fumed.

'It's for the family,' Brian explained to me gently, 'Pat, you're

14

being very selfish love.' He placed his arms around me, pointing out that there were 'a few hours in the morning for me to scribble things down. Too right I was being selfish!

'You don't just scribble things down, you have to make notes,' I tried to search out the words: Writing was my escape from drudgery. 'It's like this need, you can get inspired, and you have an urge to drop everything at any moment.'

Brian snorted. '-Reminds me of diarrhoea,' he reasoned, before pointing out some benefits. 'Besides, it's very convenient, and I hardly have to go into the office any-more.'

'You're going to work from home?!' I grimaced. He'd been having a word with his superior about E-Mailing documents over the web: Well the writing was on the wall, in the note book: Everywhere but the sodden computer screen when I heard of Brian's plans.

'Yes, well this is the computer age. We can spend more time together.'

Brilliant! I'd be mopping up after him and the kids for the rest of my life. Lazy little so and so's - and Brian only encouraged them, they hardly said, a 'hello' to me and they were back on their, on my personal computer.

**

'Right, there's going to be some changes around here.' I yelled at them the next night and I spent the next day working out a rota: A compromise, aimed at limiting the kids time on the computer and increasing mine: It went down like 'The Great Escape' on Mothers Day...

Banished: No choice, they downgraded me to kitchen table scribbles in my notebooks.

That wasn't the worst part of it though: Brian had let me down badly, siding with the kids and the off the cuff remarks that "she'd see sense in the end"? He seemed to enjoy making me feel insecure and miserable. He had changed too - later to bed each night and about as romantic, as a modem.

If there was a plus side, this was good experience for my

15

writing, yet I tapped into a side of my nature about which I would rather have not known. Working long hours with inky fingers, I wrote a novel straight from the centre of my being, a brief summary? "BORED HOUSEWIFE SEEKS ESCAPE FROM MUNDANE EXISTENCE" It was going great guns until I got to the part hard to visualise,

Henrietta sleeps with another man; Fine I could get that with Brian thinking of being with someone else was easy, anybody else, but those feelings of "escape" they were my family and I'd never needed to escape from them before - always, I found my corner and sat in it. In time I realised that escaping into myself was not enough - only something so massively tempting would take me from this drudge that was my subservient journey: How would I cope if I left Brian? To find out about myself: I'd have to leave him.

Brian learned of my plans the next morning, I rang the taxi, packed my bags and took the credit cards and some money from Brian's secret sock drawer.

Only then did hubby get nervous.

'-But you can't it's been seventeen years!' Brian bolted down the stairs; surely he'd try and stop me? I almost wished he would. We glared at each other: A return might still be possible, if Brian saw the error of his ways.

'Seventeen years, two kids,' who could hear me, I realised, 'two lovely kids and a word processor!' I screamed as I slammed the door. Getting into the taxi I reasoned that although the computer angst had shown up the cracks in this marriage, the problems had probably always been there; As my tutor would say, "the marriage had crashed..."Well it was a start and I could build on that, I'd learned a lot. After a while I caught my breath.

What would I do if I were in Henrietta's situation? It was interesting, Brian had only gone along with it to a point; When I'd made it more realistic, he'd really panicked, "there was a love in his eyes she hadn't seen in a long time - although he'd said it a lot.."

'Okay another five minutes and we'll go back.' You should have

16

seen the drivers face.

'So it was a gag?' He frowned. 'Your husband seemed very convincing...'

'-Yes, he did.' I fumbled in my purse, never one to plan well beforehand, I found that I didn't have much in the way of change.

'I suppose you've wasted my time really,' he glared at me across the passengers seat, 'with your little game-' his voice brimmed with anger. So I handed him a crumpled fifty-pound note, fresh-ish from Brian's sock drawer. He looked at it, smiled disturbingly and drove off, bemused.

'Answering questions is never a waste of time.' I smiled.

© *MARK RAYNER 1998*

notes:

My tutor liked this story – but didn't get the tag-line,

What question? He wondered – so I made sure to make it clearer in the printed version – and I moved it to first person I had all sorts of obstacles in finding a US title for this, although crossroads might have been more apt. ..

The Egg-shell Walk

'Can I bring someone?'

'Oh, a young man?' I smiled, thinking up names for my future grandchildren.

'Not exactly a "Young" man Mum, but "Jase" would love to meet you...' I could almost hear Sarah's grin.

'Well it might be a tight squeeze,' I hesitated, recalling the exact reason Sarah had stormed out of my life four years ago and gone through puberty with a nose-stud. 'You might both have to make-do with, a mattress on the floor.' Hopefully, those five little words will heal the rift - but Sarah sounds worried, there's something she wants me to know.

'Well can't you tell me at the party?'

Sarah doesn't want it to wait, she says it will be obvious the moment she walks through the door, and then, I do know, a mother *knows*.

'Sarah, save the surprise for the party.'

'Well,' she hesitates. 'I want you to know that despite everything. I love you and, I'd never do anything to hurt you.'

Curious. I repeated that I loved her too and then I slumped on the sofa with a stiff gin, stuck on Cleopatra for a girl and Cedric for a boy.

I didn't need a function hall, and most of my guests would not be staying, friction was assured from the start; my daughter and her partner had been caught "necking" in the parking bay. "Jase" had a large red Ferrari, and I looked out the window, commenting about "Boys and their toys". Sarah explained later that the passion just took them, they'd been so concerned about causing "a scene" and Sarah wanted to calm Jase's nerves.

Nothing my daughter did could shock me any-more; cigarettes, freak hair dye, offensive music and bed hopping; Yes, I'd done them all! My guests were more concerned that Jase's "parking" had forced them onto the grass bank, which in the days heavy rain now resembled the Battle of the Somme.

As it happened, I possibly couldn't have been any more shocked had Sarah turned up with her late father. Young women try to dress their partners' don't they? Well I'll give her, her due she had tried, although her hair was unkempt, blond and frizzy. I'm afraid I still had to check behind them, make sure some Adonis wasn't waiting in the wings.

My concentration settles on my daughter; my eye's radar in on her chest, then her fingers, she doesn't look as if she'll give me any more surprises.

'Oh darling, you look radiant...' I leaned forward and hugged them both and bit my tongue: I have no right to lecture my daughter on suitable partners; She has fingers and toes - she can count, fortunately her late father's numeracy skills were as lacking as his romantic ones. Sarah's eyes are begging me to ease "Jase" in gently.

'"Jase", you must think me very rude...'

'Not at all, my mother's still uneasy with us.'

So...How old are you and what do you think you are doing with my daughter? What does she see in you?

My mind is full of all these questions and Sarah's waiting for me to embarrass her; I can see it in her eyes. I take the boxed gift from them, one can never have too many glass fruit-bowls, apparently, lucky I didn't drop it.

The sitting room is strangely deserted; Six guests have vaporised! Either they're hiding behind the curtains or they are blocking the toilets. The general chitchat reveals that Sarah and Jase have been *together* for six months. "Jase" *what sort of name is "Jase"? Jase is a young man's name that's what, maybe they met in the "lonely hearts" pages. How can Sarah keep this heart from being lonely doesn't she have any respect for what my friends will think? I was knitting booties for gods' sake, now Sarah will have to keep one eye on the pacemaker...*

'Mrs Burgess. I'm sure you must know how...I love your daughter. She's indescribable.'

'"Indescribable", yes...' That's my Sarah, all right! This is just like her, to be different, to be daring, to challenge my perceptions.

An awkward silence and I can see that "look" that passes between them. 'Well, how about a nice cup of tea?' My eyes meet with Sarah's and she nods. 'I'll help you.' She leans forward and brushes Jase's cheek.

I thought she might.

'I know what you're thinking Mum,' Sarah rugby-tackles me into the kitchen. 'That I've made "a mistake", I'm confused.' Actually, I'm wondering how long that love bite on her neck will take to heal, does she have any others? Why has she come to my party wearing black, is it because she thought I'd disown her? When she says they've been together for six months...How *together* is that? Is this their first blush of passion or has the relationship ripened? I'm thinking because I don't want to *say* anything.

Lately, my relationship with Sarah has been like trying to retune a radio when the transmitter's down.

'As long as you're happy, darling,' I'm trying not to give "Jase" the chipped mug and, I really hate blue-striped wallpaper - it's time for some changes, 'and you are comfortable with Jase, I mean I wouldn't have thought that "Jase" was your...'

'-Comfortable, Mum, it feels so right.'

'Right. Does Jase take sugar?'

'-You, could ask?' Sarah sees my glare and informs me that more guests have arrived, and she'll sort out her tea. I should turn the sausage rolls down...

A familiar voice is saying that my Sarah must have been desperate.

'Melanie? How lovely, and the, er children...' My invitation clearly stated "NO CHILDREN" for just such an eventuality.

'That's right!' Her voice is almost challenging. She points to a large wrapped box, on the varnished antique circular table in the hall. 'I just bought you, a little something.' She was right.

Melanie is an erratically-dressed floral disaster, now in her early forties she kisses me like a bitch on heat.

'No, sign of Tony?' I search for her follicle-challenged husband among the shadows in the lobby.

'Um, he's just parking!' Melanie greets my daughter with a horsey smile. 'Apparently he wasn't the only one.'

Sarah blushes. Melanie seizes the moment to assure Sarah that she is a "live and let live" sort and will support her through this "phase" of her life. She wants Sarah to keep her kids occupied. Her little darlings' are clearly censored for this appearance, little blue suits on party children?

Sarah has my permission to get them as grubby as possible, by the end of the party, although it will be no easy task; they are both allergic to Ice cream and repel dirt; I learned later they were more slapdash with crayons. The smell of burning sausage meat knocked me flat...

I can hear the whispers, the sniggering and the questions and the silence when they enter a room. Unsurprisingly, Sarah and Jase have been forced onto the upstairs landing. Stupid, I should have realised, this party is crowding my daughter out. She's desperate to show Jase some affection; To sit in a chair and hold hands, yet, she's anxious not to offend our guests or get grilled by Melanie's children. This has gone far enough, I breathe deeply, is it right that Sarah and her guest should walk on eggshells in her own home? In one breath I'm suggesting that they will both be more comfortable in the master bedroom tonight.

'You don't have to do that Mum...' Sarah gently scowls at me.

'Nonsense, you've both had a long trip.' Maybe, if I had been a bit more flexible that gulf would not have existed between us. I'm touching Sarah's face, my little girl's grown up, she knows her own mind and I'm desperately proud of her.

'Mum,' Sarah follows me down the stairs. '"Jase" is uncomfortable here, we can't be ourselves when they're treating us like a, freak-show...'

'Agi dear, I'm not a prude.' Melanie glares up at me. 'It's just, there are children here and, well your daughter could be setting a better example, I mean it makes one feel quite sick.' Melanie's eyes burn with years of suppressed rage. 'To have someone you love, come into your home and, disgrace it so readily...'

Yes, it does: This, from a woman that has just allowed her kids to graffiti my beloved wallpaper.

'I think this has gone far enough...'

I'm marching my only daughter and her guest down the stairs.'Sarah, this inappropriate behaviour will have to stop.' ;The unpleasant comments: the sniggering, the pointing, the inappropriate kissing. My daughter has disgraced me for the last time. I march them up to the front door and they stand and gape at me.

'I'd like this all bought out into the open...'

I look around my circle of so-called friends, realising I may never see any of them again.

'This is Jase, my daughter's lover, and...' A gasp floats down the hall, Then, I grab hold of this irritating woman that has blighted my life - and I can't believe it, after so many years, this friend that was so important for so long is gone. I've thrown Melanie and her charming children out.

'As Melanie informed you in more colourful tones..' I hug my daughter and kiss her gently on the forehead - and her smile is like the one her father got when he won cuddly toys for her. 'I believe that's short for Jasmine....' Sarah nods.

The Wishing Well

The lamp above me lit up, bathing me in its warmth. I checked through my handbag and put some lippy on.

The regulars had been getting nervous: There were rumours of a crackdown, so it had been quiet tonight.

If I had my way, I would be wearing trainers for a fast getaway; but my colleagues said they weren't 'sexy' and could be a real turn-off. Everything was on display though; my tights were for baiting, a fisherman might envy me but the catch had to be big, the costs were high.

The rain hadn't helped; It was light but irritating. I hated getting my neck splashed; Bad enough being pushed into this kind of life, without drowning like a spider in a drainpipe.

Someone was there: He was wearing jeans and trainers with a soaking wet green coat. I noticed him first at the kerb-side. Everything about him said wet. He frowned as he came into view, looking at me in displeasure: nervous; edgy; He was insecure.

His eyes were young; like a boy in a man's body, he was wiry and I could not tell whether it was sweat or rain water splashing down his forehead; Amazing how insecure he seemed; This kind of deception would come back to haunt him as ulcers.

I felt cold enough already: within seconds rain had drenched him, his black hair dripped mercilessly as he spoke.

"I..I just need a push and something for the radiator, understand?" Following a few arrests clients had tended to request my 'services' in increasingly subdued lingo: I had heard worse, maybe cheery dripping people unnerve me, certainly I have always thought Gene Kelly was a bit of a prat.

The others were calling it quits and drifting to the late night chippy; The aroma of potatoes cooking in vegetable oil, mixing with the rain awoke my nasal passages.

"-Emm - Emma Derkett?" He grinned. His blue eyes were as watery as his hair; I shoved him into the lamp over to the side; He knew my name. Someone had obviously recommended me: That raised the price.

"I want the payment upfront...Understand? No funny business!"

He seemed bewildered, and he was trying hard not to leer at my legs; I was never that provocative - just very obvious: I still looked gorgeous; the rain may have made my face resemble a leaky tap splattered with make-up but you couldn't hide those natural assets when you were banking on them.

"Yes, of course you're on a meter are you?!"; it was then I hit him, scratching his head, like Columbo; He recoiled, wanted to know if it was something he'd said - berk!

"I'm sorry, just reflexive." I spat.

"You're very good. " He leaned nearer. "It's a bust then is it?"

He must have seen my grimace: No time for playing; First timers almost always act coy, at first then they talk dirty: This client was fooling no-one that he'd never seen a breast before, weird, I grabbed his arm, pulling him along the high street, keeping an eye on his every movement all the way back to my upstairs room.

The suspicious client even waited for me outside, he seemed over confident; anxiously I frisked him at the door, making sure he wasn't carrying anything.

"We'll call it a hundred up front and no rough stuff." My voice was at its most businesslike.

"-Very nice." The stranger sat down and dripped on my sofa. I threw him the kitchen towel and when I came into the room he was studying the photos on the table.

"Me, kid is staying with friends..." I explained sharply: A sad thing about this life: If people think you have kids they won't get too rough; Of course some people get a perve out of it, thinking how your little boy reacts when he makes his mark...

"You hated that, being called a 'kid'." He was taking in my

processions; admiring the pure white decor - was he being funny? I don't know what he was expecting: My flat told the full story: Occupied about a year the occupant having reached rock bottom with a kid and an addiction; Yet a love of her child and a tightly knit mini family to keep things stable at least; The engagement ring, the photos of Dave? A life so recent as to still be going on, somewhere in a mirror universe!

"-Mind you," my guest considered, "you hated a lot of things, Brussel Sprouts made you blotchy, spinach and you puked up butter beans!"

Where had this guy been? Was he married? Did it matter?

"You've certainly landed on your feet..."; So funny, it wasn't true: then the clincher, my guest focussed on me with deep concern."Whatever happened to Dave?"

I was stunned; No, completely gob-smacked, I'll be honest: No-one knew Dave, he was from my parallel universe; this weirdo had no right, and yet...

"You, knew Dave?"

He smiled."I remember at school, when he made bread with salt instead of flour, he couldn't make it rise." He laughed.

"I, know," I frowned.

"Does he work nights too?"

Having sat beside him, I reached lovingly for the photo frame.

"Not any-more, it was his blood," my hand brushed lovingly over the glass surface. "-Something in his blood.";Wait a moment: No, it couldn't be..."-Clive, Clive Stone?" I knew there was something about that face; He hadn't lost that boyish quality; In those last ten years since Dave had stamped on him at the leaver's party: That I shouldn't recognise him, but he sounded so different; I'd spent many innocent hours dreaming of me and Clive, my first almost love...

"You're not in the habit of taking total strangers into your flat are you?" Clive was appalled.

Dim or what? I knew them very well after a few 'sessions': Talking of which...

"-Better take a shower, you'll catch pneumonia, else."

He seems unsure. "I'm not keeping you from anything, am I?" He really is nervous. This turned out to be the quickest shower in history; maybe he thought I had someone else, waiting?

"Do you have a hair dryer?" Clive asks through a brief gap in the door: Vain or what? He'll only get it wet again later - much later; I have to admit I've got my doubts about this; We've known each other all our school lives: But time is money - and he asked for me by name, for a moment I'm almost sad: Clive was special, an undented Mr Perfection, I'm not sure I could ever sleep with someone that wanted to go with a prostitute, how can you tell someone that you don't want to sleep with them? How far should I go? With Clive and me it had been so different: A kissy, huggy love building from them moments spent on each other's lips, we'd have spent days in each other's throats: before all those complicated bits got in the way, with Dave it was all about performance; Trouble was that he bored us both rigid when he bought his ego into our bed.

"I didn't want to say anything earlier..." Clive's quickly made his way into the kitchen: I've chucked the sweeteners behind the flowerpot and reasoned he can have Dave's old mug. "You got in then? Never -have guessed."

"Sorry, what?" He'd caught me by surprise, rubbing a tear for yesterday from my eye.

"It's an undercover job?" He asked, taking my silence as an indication he had spoilt a surveillance operation. Clive explained that taking my tough exterior seriously was impossible for him; He'd seen me crying when a boy kissed me in the playground and seen me cowering when mum shouted at me: A long time ago maybe; I was still so delicate and feminine, and when I spoke, I slipped into subdued welsh-tones: All this leather clobber was a lie I was telling everyone: or maybe only myself.

"Well this has been nice," Clive reached for the door and made one last survey of the room before retrieving his coat from the bathroom.

"You, must be very cold dressed like that." He commented.

"It can be a bit degrading," I nod blankly, "but it gets results..."

He agrees; : "Well, Emm-, I wish you well..." He stops "Be careful too," he added, placing the lightest kiss we ever had on my cheek."People might think you really are, well don't take this the wrong way, but I'd never be able to tell the difference..."

26

I was glaring at him quite coldly: He backed into the wall calendar.

Clive stops: It's as if he has just worked out a joke that had been puzzling him. "I just realised. You could have got the wrong idea and arrested me for kerb-crawling!" He reached for a milk bottle from the sink and filled it.

"That will do," Clive rolls a new pound coin across the kitchen table. "'One hundred' you said, wasn't it?"

After he'd gone, I went to the bathroom: His wallet greets me out of the corner of my eye; He was always absent minded at school: Went home in the wrong coat - twice. In that moment, I can see that little girl in the mirror that took him in hand and kissed him at least twice: on special occasions; I'm forced to wonder how things might have changed if things were different; He was never my man. Within the wallet, was at least one hundred and fifty pounds and a cashpoint card; I would return the wallet to the police station first thing in the morning: I had that bizarre feeling that Clive had seen right through me...

© 1998/2001

Notes:

I quite liked Emma – a vulnerable character with a mysterious past and it's true she wasn't well drawn and her accent was terrible – so after having an early version rejected by Bella I left it there – a year or so later when I wrote a sitcom idea for BBC Talent I needed some stories for my five years of plots section – so, taking Clive from the sitcom I added him to the old story – and I doubt you can even see the join – or can you? The back-story for Sarah comes because of BBC Talent – but in that case, it first was offered for the Richard and Judy Short Story Competition...

Do You Remember Me?

It was just another Saturday night. Marie sighed into her pasta. The highlight of her week had been getting the new cat neutered. That bad, eh? Well yes, the closest she had come to being swept off her feet was in the hurricane.

A little romance, a nice meal...

"Just for once..." Marie sighed.

Then the phone rang.

"Em. Is that M Dawson?"

A male voice. Marie was at first, intrigued, then furious: Her number was supposedly ex-directory.

"Yes?" She pondered as the cat nibbled on her ankle.

"Do you remember me? I remember you..."

Marie so wanted to recall the cheery tones, he sounded so alive: How she longed to make a connection.

"Oh yes," Marie coughed, her mind still a blank.

"You were a freckly-thing, with braces when I saw you last..." The voice paused.

"Refresh my memory..." Marie insisted.

"-Jeremy Adams, Class of '74?" Another longer pause before he added meekly. "I used to pull your ponytails..."

Marie could just see him, double chin and evil little piggy-eyes.

"Horrid little, boy!" Marie smiled warmly, although her voice lost its cultured tones: as for a second she was back in the playgrounds of her youth and she always recalled the coldness of playing netball, rather than socialising with her peers. "That's it, do it again!" Jeremy laughed. Finally, Jerem recovered, aware he may have lost his audience. "Anyway, the reason I'm ringing is that next Saturday we've got a get-together at the old school - 'The fences?'"

Silence.

"You do remember where it is?"

Marie fell silent. A picture in her mind of that frightened little girl with the rosy knees covered in battle-scars. Had she been crying?

Just got sore eyes...

Another hug from her big sister: "M, however, did you get this gunk in your hair, you smell like a toilet?"

You tell your big sister all about it...

"Yes, I remember..."

Another laugh.

"I've had terrible trouble tracking you down, but your Uncle Frederick gave me your number."

"Did he?" Marie squirmed. Well that was a kick in the shin for Uncle Fred if he ever showed up again.

"I tell you what Em, I'll pick you up at your place next Saturday?"

Marie nodded, before remembering Jeremy couldn't see her. He was certainly persistent.

"Okay, fine." Marie sounded underwhelmed.

"Great, will be brilliant seeing you again," Jeremy breathed in. "We had a bet going that no-one would find you, some of us even thought you were dead."

The sad thing was they were right, M Dawson had become a recluse and the little girl they all remembered was long dead, Marie couldn't protect her any more but she could exorcise a ghost from her past and she promised herself that she would certainly let her hair down next Saturday night...

By that next Saturday, Marie had cruised the shops for that special outfit and having not been able to find one, she had selected a dark-green dress suit with white gloves.

A search of the Internet had produced some juicy facts to enliven those dull gaps in conversation between the peanuts and the tuna sandwiches. Marie had even bought her cat some extra special sachets in respect of his forthcoming housekeeping duties. Having prepared for all occurrences, she still hadn't expected to find a white limo at her doorstep.

"Hello, Jeremy?" They kissed, only socially, pleasant enough if you excused the peppermint. Jeremy contrasted quite visibly with the image in her minds' eye: His eyes were puffy and bloodshot. His blue striped suit covered an indulgent stomach and he carried a gold-topped walking cane.

The years had not been kind to Jeremy

"Just my leg," Jeremy cheered, "I had a little accident, a while back."

"-How dreadful for you."Marie paused.

"-I still dance though." Jeremy grinned: His teeth were capped. His hair was ginger and long, it sat as if uncomfortable, almost glued to his head...

Oh.

By journey's end, Jeremy had made seven attempts to clasp Marie's hand: He was a tactile person who had lost his tact.

"It must have cost a fortune to hire the limo driver," Marie smiled.

"-It was worth it for you," he coughed, "I've always had a soft-spot for..."

"-Don't spoil it." Marie let Jeremy edge-back into the beige upholstery.

"Hey everyone, look who's turned up. It's 'Em'!" Jeremy chirped as he escorted Marie from the limo. Marie blushed, she had not expected to be put on public display, and she now realised that her dress and shoes clashed terribly - in fact the dress highlighted her cheekbones. She stood waiting for another uncertainty to strike her: but instead, she was rugby-tackled into the bar by an overly affectionate gripping woman.

"Em, lovely to see you,"

Marie looked blank.

"Julie?" The woman attempted to reheat the warmth between them. "Julie Oliver?"

While Marie tried to take in all of those faces, Julie unburdened her of her coat. Marie was sucking on a disappointingly flat fruit cocktail when Julie returned.

"God, you haven't changed!" Julie exclaimed, "well a bit older of course," she backed off, "but then, we all are..."

Marie smiled.

"-So, after that, I got a job at that Elenby Road shoe shop, had to leave, ladders you know?" Julie was in her stride now.

"-In, your tights?" Marie almost made a joke: Julie convulsed like a cat with a fur-ball. "-No, going up ladders."

Marie had known that: This was her attempt at humour. Jeremy was grunting in her direction as 'Agadoo' invaded the loud speakers.

*

"-So, Em. Did you ever get married?" Jeremy winked, he'd saved the 'Careless Whisper' instrumental version, just for her: Strange how men walked on your dreams.

"No," she shook her head resolutely, "I was engaged but it didn't work out..."

Jeremy's eyes widened."So, you're still looking for someone to keep your bed, you, warm at night?"

Marie coughed: That reminded her."Oh no," she beamed, hoping to appear mysterious, "One male in my life is very good at that..."; Although, the male in question was probably out ratting; It was amazing how people resembled their pets...

An hour later and Marie called it a night: That final trip to the little girl's room had done it; Worn face muscles and that crafty, grey streak which had chosen now to dangle from her forehead: Reunions make you feel old.

"We must stay in touch." Julie hugged her. Marie decided that she would.

"We will," Julie assured her, "how about next week, that little bar round the corner?"

Marie agreed.

"You're a revelation!" Julie shook her head in disbelief.

"How do you mean?" Marie put her coat on.

"Well, there's no way I'd socialise with someone who used to pull my hair, stick my head down the toilet and pinch me," Julie edged her aside, "-and you never told big Sis, either? That's the thing I couldn't get. She was a year older, she'd have made, you know she'd have fixed him,"

"She probably wouldn't have had time for me," Marie rubbed away a tear.

"-Probably, she was, well you have to agree. A bit of a cow, wasn't she? I mean, not to be disrespectful or anything..."

Marie frowned: "Yeah, she was. So he took my dinner money too?"

"-And, bus fare, but I suppose that's all in the past?"

Marie allowed a smile to cross her face.

"We must do this again sometime," Jeremy leered at her. Marie nodded, searching his eyes for meaning. "Look, the night's young and we're both adults..."

Marie edged off: She was at just the right distance to separate the differing smells of Jeremy: Alcohol and breath.

Jeremy smiled, "I've always known you fancied me, I'm very observant..." He smarmed and brushed her knee.

"Oh, you weren't that observant Jeremy..." Marie bit her tongue, "you see we've never actually met."

Jeremy glared coldly: What did she mean?

"Oh, I saw you about, same school but it was my Sister Emma that was in your class,"

Jeremy became uncomfortable, he eased back as far across the backseat as he could.

Marie became agitated. "That's why she abbreviated it to 'Em'" she pounced, "my parents' lacked imagination which is where I don't get it from. I fancied a night out, to meet some people," she explained: "funny how 'Em' didn't talk much about how you bullied her..." Marie made a lunge for Jeremy's head: In an instant, she'd scalped him of his ginger toupe launched from the car window into an oily puddle outside.

Then, Marie swiped his wallet, removing a solitary ten-pound note, for flowers.

The last thing Jeremy heard above the sound of his driver's laughter was the determined tones of Marie Dawson.

"-Us, M Dawson's have to stick together!" She yelled before hailing a cab and speeding away:

Marie wiped a solitary tear from off her face: relief she suspected at her narrow escape and realisation that her little sister had lived her life to the full, despite the 'Jeremy's' of this world: If Emma could have been there she'd have done the same thing: Marie would never have had this much fun staying at home.

© MARK RAYNER 1999/2001

Dedicated to the memory of David Rayner who indirectly inspired this tale, through a number of auspicious phone calls.

Notes: Don't write about reunions goes the saying – they're a cliché – only it really wasn't like that. My Uncle got a call inviting me to a reunion at Mark Hall School in Essex – only when I investigated, it was actually an invite for another Mark Rayner who had been there in 1971 when I was a year old.

So I came up with this tale. It was only later that I read about the rule on Twist in the Tale reunions – and by then the story was at Bella, where their fiction Editor had sent me a lovely letter saying that although there was 'much in the story that she liked'. She didn't feel that it was right for Bella – I agreed; but at the time Bella was pretty much the only market for male writers – eventually I prepared a re-edit for Crystal, then I found out about the 'rule' so I saved a couple of quid and got on with something else...

Journey of Life

My name is Robert Wyre, with a "y" not an "i"; there is never usually the time for me to sit and wallow: but then just then as I bought my ticket for this train, I recalled the gentle click of dinner money; you would hold it in your moistening palm: and in return they'd give you this pathetic strip of segments one for each day. By the end of the week you'd be left with this silly little orange bit; woe betide anybody who lost it....

I don't normally go by train: but, "the office" is having a "leave your car at home" day! It came at the worst possible time, but these things always do: I'm forty-ish; I worry about my health that's expected, but worrying about making your connection? Last thing I need, specially now.

One of our best men has been "approached" shall I say? James has been with my company since I opened the place: he's more like a family friend than a worker: good at his job too; it's sad: he will obviously stay at Wyre Printers and Packers, he has been with us for twenty-five years; He knows which side his bread is buttered, which reminds me, my wife's packed me some sandwiches here, somewhere.

What would, I give for some toast?! Well never mind: I'm dying for a fag too: but Anthony and Kevin are sat a few carriages down, and I never smoke in front of my employees: not when they're on a health-kick anyways: they call him "Ant" you know: I never thought he'd work out: he has a pin in his nose and an earing; Kevin has a tattoo on his arm of a dragon! Scruffy devils they used to be, so I put my foot down, made them at least wear tidy shirts - Kev said: "We should wear proper footwear too!" So I made him the health and safety chap: and he lands me with a bill for a thousand quid, for safety clothing!

When I was at school, it was shirt and tie, none of this "earing" stuff: I was proud to wear it; actually I lie. I loathed the tie: it was a drab purple-striped thing, I remember making a walk home - tearing the bloody thing off, chucking it into my bag, which was always packed solidly: thinking on it, I never used to pack my school-bag; I used to keep all my books in there all the time! I suppose that's why my back went!

Two sugars? This is nice...so anyway, this uniform: this hideous purple jumper and this embarrassing tie; they may as well have made us wear our testicles' around our necks - it wouldn't have been any the less humiliating; You can just picture me. I had glasses. I was a swot; looking back, I loathe him; I never developed at school because I loved it! I was a smart-young, well-behaved, impeccable, see? See how that image leaps into your mind's eye: the impeccable gentleman, and that meant I never lived up to my full potential; mind you - how could you enjoy school-life, when you spent your days dashing from class to class, and your nights panicking about that piece of homework.

I used to loathe homework; I learnt late that homework consisted of catching up on the stuff that bored you into a coma in your classes; it was better to get it over with, in your lunch-break. I loved English but I struggled with Maths and French, so, they put me in remedial classes for them.

They couldn't understand why I was so good at English, yet so bad at other less creative subjects: it was the teachers, that was why.

At my school the whole class had detention every night even when only one person (never me) played up. So I got used to them, although I was the "Bobby Ewing" of my classroom...

Well, there was also a point system; two negative points meant detention - but they were cancelled out by positive points. I would spend my day collecting "possies" like a butterfly: it was the French teacher who set me up - he tore my wing. He had told me to leave a piece of homework I couldn't manage, but next day he changed his mind: he challenged me about why I had left it.

"Well that's a negative point!' He yelled: I was befuddled, it would have been a miscarriage of justice but there was no justice at that frigging school: so, I remember looking at him and I got this cold-warm feeling in the pit of my gut and all my respect I held for this linguist: it bubbled away and I hated that man leaning over me in the garish snazzy green suit: I loathed him with the only energy I had to keep me from collapsing. Sometimes, people stay in your mind; I'm not so bitter now, I realise he was just a prat...

I can always tell when someone isn't going to be able to work with us; I try never to gauge by appearance alone, "Bob on a Wyre" they called me:

until my blood pressure became toxic, when it became, "Bob on a diet." - That's quite funny: thing-is, I look like that French teacher now, greying, bulging: a prat...

I should never have taken the train today: should have parked a few blocks down: I can usually find the energy for deviousness when I need it. So anyway, I got lucky, I found some old magazines on a spring fair stall that weekend before D Day: detention day, "Look and Learn" I think they were called.

The plan was simple: I would collect together the many volumes and take them into school and get a positive point. Sad really, I got my first "possie" doing a poem based on the work of Esther; a real artist who made recursive paintings that looked in themselves - weird, in religious education, it was: my first draft just couldn't do justice to this picture, so I began to rewrite it. The teacher went along and read it, said I had "Beautifully captured the recursive effect of the work!" Anyway that was my first "possie". So anyway, I planned to hand over the magazines to the remedial teacher first thing Wednesday morning - well she scoffed, dismissed me, "Can you bring them back later?"; So I had to hump this sweaty bag of old magazines as well as my ordinary overloaded school bag from class to class...

My afternoon class was art: The teacher once called me a genius when I managed to paint an orange with all the right textures - no, I don't know what she was on either: but, she brushes back her long golden locks.

"Oh is that scrap-paper for the art-block?" She smiles - I'm a little caught out by this. I had expected to cheer the remedial class with something for us to copy our drawings from; but all of a sudden I realise: I don't like remedial class very much: they took me from

36

my friends, their all or nothing, if you have maths weaknesses you must be bad at English too: put 'em all in the same boat, watch 'em drown mentality; and I realise that Art is the only class where I'm not under threat, so I grit my teeth sadly and hand over the moist plastic bag.

"These are great, well I think that's worthy of a positive point!" She beams: and then this girl from my class who I will love forever explains about the French Teacher; the miscarriage of justice, - and my art teacher cancels out my "neggy" with a "double possie" and I could kiss her...

You see, the practical side of things doesn't matter a jot when you've got everyday concerns, I realised that day: if the offer was good then I could be unpredictable: those magazines were gone; they should have ended their days lent on and traced out on a pile by the Encyclopaedia Britannica's, instead they would splash out with varying coloured paints within the next week. Did I care? I was in the black, a little sad about the lost magazines, no? Well, yes but a lot happier than if they'd given me an official detention. I realised later, when I was laying back on my bunk and counting my often unlucky stars - that school had played me for a sucker. So I didn't turn up for class detentions after that, and if I was a few minutes late for class, then tough!

And so we arrive: our journey is at an end, big waste of time it has been too; but I think I'll make our lad a better offer: too late, maybe, but I'd like to make a deal to keep him with us. I know he's loyal and that he might not even consider their proposal - but I can't take that risk, because he might be unpredictable...Like-what, I am.

© 2002

Thank You Charlotte Adams!

"Mad Charlotte," we called her at school.

If there was a tree to climb, a ladder to perch on - then chatty Charlotte would blooming well perch on it, she had a lovely disposition - and, though I say it myself she was a distinguished rare breed even sexier wearing glasses; She was just relieved for the near miss with that Bunsen burner - that flare altered the pigment of her left eye and her green eye twinkled in my envy.

She developed breasts before the rest of us had even found Channel Five; I was always shadowed by her: her lanky 'mate'.

Charlotte captained our netball team - I hated her for that! You've never seen someone recover so quickly from such a serious sprain - and hobble back to take the trophy: and be nominated as class rep for refusing to be side-lined - Bitch! Always with our best interests at heart - She'd stand at the front of the class piercing the blackboard for effect as we heard third hand what they'd decided for us at their 'hush, hush' meeting.

As for boyfriend's - well I wasn't interested in her love life, Adam would have been mine if he hadn't became tangled in Charlotte's intricate little web, still she was welcome to him nesting in her ginger dandruff - thanks to evidence of the locker room, I was only too aware of her true colours so to speak.

I tried to like her - even sharing a banana after she toppled in the canteen - one of her fad diets had nearly killed her: but backstabbing and bitching was not my style: I left that to sickly Charlotte - only once did I really let her have it, it was a wet Wednesday and god alone knows why but we were discussing careers in our English lesson.

'I always thought I'd set up my own business!" Charlotte announced, placing both hands behind her neck.

'Yeah,' I grinned, all my co-horts eyes upon me, 'people will pay good money for your services!'

'No,' Charlotte turns yet another colour in objection, 'Not, that..'
She glares back at me.

'Car cleaning?' I suggested was what I'd been thinking, 'I can
see you crawling down in the back seat,' I smirked, adding, 'I always
saw you as a little scrubber.'

Adam winks in her direction, 'Well you can climb my ladder any
time!' He says.

Well alarms must have rung, those thought processes buzzing
'cause six months out of school and I've just been kicked off my
apprenticeship - and I see Charlotte in the small ads; I'd heard she'd
got engaged by then and even bungy-jumped naked on her
honeymoon - I shouldn't be surprised.

FEMALE WINDOW CLEANER

'Who'd of thought it.'

'Make's sense,' Mum smiles at me, 'Who wants a man to do it,
peering in at your unmentionables...'; Mum supposed that women are
more sure footed in their career paths, and she's surprised that I
didn't think of it.

So how did I feel when I saw news of that terrible tragedy right
there in black and white barely a week later?

How did it feel to have a best friend who I'd helped up that
ladder to success by way of that sarky conversation in fifth form, the
lady with the chamois and green bucket always out on the street, as
befitted her: but with this mile high smile and soapy water suds
splashing down each arm; self contented, confident sexy Charlotte -
who'd even expanded to Satellite dishes and Tv ariels last time I saw
her the girl with no fear - until her ladder wobbled. Let's just say
that when I saw the opportunity I was glad of the chance that I was
given to give her a nudge in the right direction.

Well, it's six months on - and do I still feel guilty about what happened? Well, to be honest - I'm bitter! Charlotte's cheery features still plague my memories - and that image of her smashed on the ground like crockery at a Greek wedding - Splat!

How many people do you know could get up from that? They say: "She's a true hero." Charlotte's thrown aside that sickly green livery and her shattered limbs; She's apparently animatronic now, all smiles, and she's coaching the local wheelchair Basket Ball team! When she isn't scoring! Their baby looks just like her husband, Adam, apparently they're "Closer than ever," and she's feeling "Very Lucky!"

I hate you Charlotte Adams!

© 2004

Notes; Sometimes a story is just right – you see a market but it can't be made to fit – but it just doesn't feel riight to alter it, with Moving on the biggest problem was the word 'bitch'.

Fortunately, some overseas markets wouldn't have minded; but there was just the tiny matter of the 50% tax rate for not being an Australian tax payer..charming.

Moving On

'Oh, you're not, taking the light-bulbs, you're being ridiculous love!'

Don't know why: they're my light-bulbs; special long life ones and I haven't had my money's worth. How dare he call me "ridiculous" in front of my son? ; Speaking of which, peering into the bathroom, I see that Geoff's persuaded Robert to clean the bath.

'Nearly done Mum,' Rob smiles at me: he's so like his dad, I wish he wasn't wearing trainers though; they will ruin the enamel, still not my problem, I must remember the loo-roll holder. Mum got me that, and Andrew's portrait: it used to be in the Master Bedroom: but Geoff had "issues" with it: said it was off-putting. I think that's now down in the gap beside the airing cupboard.

'That'll teach you, to have one-last shower.'; I frown as Geoff appears, carrying a large brown box. 'You know we're supposed to be out by twelve?'

'That reminds me,' Geoff smiles coyly. 'I understand the new place has thicker walls...' Robert squirms as Geoff caresses my back Robert carries the black soapy bucket from the bath to the landing, muttering.

'That was way too much information!' He's gone all red.

I take a last look out at the garden. There's an Uncle Walter rose I wanted to take and probably some spuds as well.

'That's alright Mum,' Robert takes the bucket from the windowsill. 'I'll be staying at Jessie's tonight. So you-two, can have the house to yourselves...'; He's so grown up now; I sometimes forget, and he misses his dad In the garden at the back, there's this old swing frame, it collects thistles now, but it used to be important.

' That's the upstairs done...' Geoff growls.

'-And the bathroom is spotless?'

'Yes.'

'No-more messy fingerprints, are there?' He has to show me one last time, just so I can make sure. '-The Portrait, the one of Andrew?'

41

'-Fran, you saw me pack it...' he grabs my hands, 'Now-you don't have to visit the bathroom again?'

'Yes, and I'll need a screwdriver!' I bustle back in.

'Mum what's up?' Robert calls from the middle step.

'Just this thing your Mother's got for personal hygiene...'

'This thing'; Obsessive Compulsive Disorder is the medical term for it: had to think of something to explain the frequent trips to the bathroom; Geoff must never know...

'I'm taking Sandy out then!' Robert calls back, and the back door slams as they leave: Sandy, our dog is a cross-breed: Alsatian-Staffordshire: mix them together and you get the softest mutt; like Geoff, a pussy cat really.

My heart jumps a beat as Geoff's mobile rings from the living room; we had to lose the land-line yesterday: I've never felt so isolated, I panic that I haven't cancelled the papers. Geoff's chatting to his Mum. Don't know what she'll do without him.

'Yes Mum, the new number as soon as we're settled.'

'I've got it somewhere,' I dash to the kitchen, knowing the message board left with the cutlery. I return dejected. I can't remember it: not now.

'Sorry!'

Geoff assures her he'll pass it on and tells me to try and relax. 'Still a good hour,' he smiles, patting the last box of my books on the kitchen table. 'Why don't we have a last cup of tea?' I explain that I've packed the herbal ones. Geoff says that's okay, and we stand alone, him hugging me in this kitchen for the last time...

'You don't think Robert still blames me, do you?' I ask.

Geoff is surprised. 'No, I'm sure that's not the case. There can't be many mothers willing to move, somewhere new, for their son's business...'

But I'm still not sure, Geoff faces me more seriously. 'Remind me again, what the Coroner said.'

'That he, Andrew had-'

'-That Andrew had high blood pressure and a heart defect,' Geoff recalls.'-Nothing you did would have made any difference, even in a healthy marriage.'; I wish I could believe that: but you see I did know about Andrew's heart: he wanted to live an active life and I

42

wasn't about to stop him; a little extra salt here; some over exertion there; Andrew was like an overgrown teenager, convinced, he was immortal. He was advised to change his eating habits. The silly old fool never took any notice of his Doctor: Geoff's right: it's not right for me to wallow in "What If's".

Geoff kisses me and clasps my hand.

'-But,'

'-No butts - a new start, remember?' Geoff reminds me, then he kisses me again and cups my face.

'A new start...' I agree. Moving away, it seems so final, like I'm leaving Andrew as well as our home, we've been here so long; all our friends are here, but the sacrifice will be worth it. Geoff's invested a lot in our future - and I know things will soon pay off.

I'm about to kiss Geoff back: but Robert's returned with Sandy. He's standing apprehensively in the kitchen: and so he's here again: the only one that knows the truth, no wonder he wants to keep away, he knows that tonight Geoff and I will christen the new bedroom and life will move on: strange, he gets on so well with Geoff: that can sometimes be awkward, can't it, coping with new members of the family? He's the only one that knows about 'Daddy's' special medicine - and there's always the risk... So I'll begin again, raising the pressure day by day: there had to be someone for me to confide in, so I told him about it. He was shocked at first, but I think he understood: but, one day he'll blab probably to that little bitch on the estate.

It's something I never thought I'd have to do.

'The lads say if you're putting the kettle on they wouldn't say no!' Geoff announces to us before his last reccy: I bet they wouldn't! We're a bit low on cups but we should just manage it if Rob doesn't mind being "Mother".

Geoff says the kitchen table will have to be dismantled and go in the back seat because there's no room on the van. Brilliant! I've got to take the keys around as well. Robert promises he'll dig up the rose if I can find the remote control. We're soon down on our knees by the cooker looking for a note book and perhaps a pen that's dust coloured.

43

Then, all I'll have to do is to wash up the cups. Speaking of which, there's one member of our household looking dehydrated with an expectant smirk and a wagging tail. I search for his bowl in the cupboard but all I have left is the pavlova dish full of crumbs, which I tip into the sink. Sandy sprints forward, happily, sloshing the liquid down.

Suddenly, Sandy flinches, looking at me; as if he's accusing me; his paws outstretched: staring questionably at his dish. Geoff returns, giving Sandy an odd look. He's wondering what's up. He says Sandy can't be pining. We haven't even left yet. He's reminded to take the basket and towels from the hoover-cupboard under the stairs: then he remembers the magazines and my few pairs of shoes. I'm just going upstairs for a last look around to double check that I haven't left any plant pots, net-curtains, or dirty cups, when

Robert calls me back.

'Mum!' Robert despairs. He's worked out what's wrong with Sandy. 'You know he doesn't like sugar in his tea!'

'Oh, silly me...'; I'd thought it was the smell of the pie dish that Sandy didn't like.

Robert shakes his head. 'You used to make that mistake with dad as well, so I had to drink it.' Robert wonders whether all that extra tea was good for his bladder.

'No dear, I don't suppose it was..'

© 2002

44

LIVING WITH THE FUTURE:

A long time ago in an I.T room far, far away there was this word processor with a novel lying dead on its hard-drive; I'd saved it as I went; but now it was going to need retyping onto the new computer and that included Chapter 16 which had taken the longest to write and was now lost forever; I realised somewhere around the third draft that the story was a mess – the plot and the notes I'd made just couldn't be rescued.

My local WH Smith was selling copies of the Sci-Fi fantasy publication Interzone – and I realised that I could take the two main characters from the novel and place them into an Interzone style short story to make up for the work I'd done creating the characters.
I developed an opening gambit of James Bond/Macgyver proportions.

I received a lovely letter back from Interzone – they liked the story but it didn't make enough sense – although it had a good 'feel' "my oblique approach kept the reader too far away from the action – it was promising but puzzling,"

These comments were gold-dust ; I changed the viewpoint characters and reworked the tale. Derva Rising was my first online submission and it will always hold a special place – various US titles considered it over the next couple of years and one noting it was too long for them at the moment begged me to be of good cheer and please continue my fine literary efforts," so I did, and the novel?

Well having finally been finished in 2003, I re-edited it and sent it off - the first response was so quick that I took the very wise decision to leave it in the drawer.. but in this world of self publication – I doubt that Andrew and Amy will be quiet for long..

Derva Rising

"Can you hear them? Can you hear them coming?" Hencho grabs at my shoulder, he is like a panicked child, clinging although the span of his hand is too small and he knows I will pull him away.

"I can. The Sergeant could. He went mad, you know?" I know.

"Hencho..." I don't know how to calm him, I never knew. I just blink and then he is running away across the sand, always running blindly: I pray he never saw what killed him: later that evening I realised that Hencho would not be coming back. Having crawled on knees and hands as far as I could, I then realised I had gone too far, and that my many wounds (which Hencho had so solemnly bathed) were reinfected: and now, I was going nowhere.

I have been alone (apart from the sound of my enemies' gunfire) on Derva Six for five days and I hate it. This planet has become a wilderness of craters, hard lumpy chasms which suck men into the pools below; like taking refuge on a chocolate digestive before it is dunked in hot frothing liquid...and why am I thinking of chocolate? A forest of implosions from the sky: yes, Derva Six is a forest of bombs. I have classified each hissing gnat, each swishing branch under the title 'Paranoia'. The insect life here still gnaws at me, then they die, awash in my blood: their future generations never learn, I might pity them if I was not so drowsy...

Sometimes, I sit and rest, I fall asleep, my only way out of here, even if only in day dreams: in my mind's eye I can still make love, in my dreams I still have hope. I'll see my sweet Cardilla and the beautiful dwelling in perfect white that would have housed our next generation - had the Derva not come and burnt it.

We lost it all.

I lost it all. I still have this box, my Commander's secret weapon.

My commander said it would win the war - but he stayed out in the sun too long. He was a white-haired crusty man, a weak man: his plan was of such precision on our battle map: but there was a weak link - himself. I cannot even get the box somewhere to detonate it. The irony is my lowly rank made the contents unknown to me and now my colleagues are gone...

Suddenly the air breezes with expletives and I clasp my battle scars, hoping the Derva let me die with dignity: Maybe I should throw myself in front of their lasers?

*

We found the soldier clasping at his chest, his face, wretched; it was as if he'd been there for some time. My colleague, Amy's visitation was more acrimonious, the air breezed with expletives. We must have looked an horrific sight: Amy, naked clasping her arm and glaring at the soldier through gritted teeth: myself, dressed in a bloodstained white suit from another war in another world: it is time to check the patient's dexterity.

"Um, Andrew Cuthbert!" I clasp at my suitcase, dropping it where he can see it, directly in front of him on the crisp undergrowth. "Suitcase! Hey! Foreign devil! The girl has a flesh-wound..."; if he were able to move my outburst would surely rouse him. As I watch, his eyes flicker and he observes me through his delirium. "You do too," I consider, "all right, we better get you undercover..." Amy thinks we should patch his wounds before we move him: she eases the suitcase open.

"Well?"

"Warm..." She smiles at me.

"Success!" I switch on the Geographic Analyser for destination and detail, as Amy crawls undignifiedly over our patient: a sensation he seems to be enjoying, he clutches at her head in dismay.

"Hey!"

"Red!" He pulls at a strand from her scalp, fiercely so as to snap it from her crest.

"Ow!" She berates him.

"-Red, like blood. My eyes, must be my eyes!"

"What's he rambling about now?" I ask her, before leaning across to check his pupils; "You've spent too long in the Dervan sun but yes, Amy's hair is red. It's a Martakian quirk! And I wouldn't

47

pull it again, understand?"

Amy tugs me away. "He's just suffering PTS, heightened sense of alert." A look crosses her face and her eyes chill me. "Andrew, we've been dropped straight in the middle of the Dervan War..." She can probably feel my arm tremble.

"-How do you know it's the middle?" I realise what I have said as those words escape me; dully, I note the tiresome glint in her eyes. "Oh yes of course..." Pointing the analyser at our patient, makes him reluctant. I would like to calm him but I can't get the hang of this smiling, I never could. "I apologise, my fellow, but if I attempted communication in your tongue: I'd get a gob full of phlegm, and you'd be washing your hair for the next week."

"Human..." He smiles. The assumption takes me by surprise. Meanwhile, he absent-mindedly smears his hand down my jacket: this action does not endear him to me. "Well it's always useful to learn a second language..."

At this, Amy stumbles painfully forward. "Hi, Amy Alison," she finishes patching the wounds tightening the bandage around his chest: he appears to only be focussed on her; later he will tell us of his love, Cardilla; they were, of flesh, young lovers around the same age as Amy appears. (Amy appears as a twenty-five-year-old of a healthy build, homely in a distant alien kind of way.)

For now, our immediate priority was to get him to base, Amy briefly pulled a piece of local flora - a crisp blackened leafy vegetation for analysis...

***

Dusty packets of bandages and uneasy bottles of fluid fight for dominance on the long narrow table. The soldier explains that this is the room where their Commander stood in contemplation, brushing his greying moustache and digging at an aggravating tooth.

I venture their commander resembles me, although Amy counters that he probably did not have blood in his graying beard. The soldier reasons that I resemble a gnome, he is not the first to point this out and I soon tire of this pettiness. He says that the map at the side of the room was once stabbed with pins and slithers of cardboard, before, in his words, 'The Derva blew it all away.'

The table and the polished wood chairs are sprayed in dust; a chess set also died in battle; the game will never be completed, for the soldier cannot play.

"Please, make yourself...My home?" He stammers. Amy scurries through the suitcase looking for clothing. Her body is still heavily-scarred. One of her arms is partially placed in a sling; although judging from the way, she carried him in here, her deformity does not affect her strength.

"I feel like a perishing womble!" She grins at the patient, but he does not understand the sentiment. "Maggots....," Amy explains, opening a plastic container. "I'm sorry, I don't use insecticides," she smiles, "could never get them through customs..."

The wounds are soon cleaned: the soldier seems horrified at first, then they tickle as they nourish themselves on the decomposing flesh and soon, he relaxes.

"No," I frown, catching her look, "well maybe outside..."

Before she can react, the soldier pulls at her arm. "Cardilla?"

"Amy!" She reminds him, edgily.

"You-so, remind me of my Cardilla. You are my strength, seeing me battered into human meccano, by the Derva's inept target practise."Amy hands him a metallic cup. The contents singe her fingers: she won't let him drink it, just dabs it on his lips; In time, the liquid will search through the slime and into his throat and the liquid is warming. He soon tires, slumping onto her arm. She steadies his head and waits as he drifts away...

"Well?" Amy leaves our sanctuary to meet me in the forest."Not really, no!" She can see me fuming because, yes I did manage to get the casing open and the scattered remains of the 'theoretically-timed' explosive have left me chilled.

"Remind me again .What is our mission?"

"To, end the war on Derva?" Amy offers, 'to find a peaceful solution to the Dervan War.."

"-Not fundamentally the same thing," I speculate.

"The history books they say, the war on Derva never

49

happened...The reason for the battle was lost in the-,"

"-Mists of time?"

"Yes," where these things usually are. Finally, I can show Amy the intricate workings of the explosive box. "If this thing had gone off, we'd have what their commander termed 'a stalemate': too much explosive, the entire planet vaporised before you can say 'I surrender!'"

"That's their solution?" Amy sees me nod, "What about the position of the two aggressors?"

"That's easy..." I lead Amy a little way into the forest. Now that the protective air stream has dodged us, she can smell death all around us," The position of the soldiers is, spread-eagled; if it ever was a suicide mission, they soon lost heart for it..."

"-And the Derva?"

"Well I was about to come to that..."

***

"This planet has become a wilderness of craters which suck men into the pools below: like taking refuge on a chocolate digestive before it is   dunked in hot frothing liquid...and why am I thinking of chocolate?"

"Provocative isn't it?"

Amy frowns, glaring at the computer screen."Yes..." She admitted. "How did you know where to find his computer records?"

"Ah," I ponder, "well computers are common. I guessed they'd be some record..."

"-You've been here before?"

"What makes you say that?" Pressing a button, I highlight a section of the screen. "What does, 'hard lumpy chasms sucking men into their very pools,' mean to you? And please keep it decent..."

"Earthquakes?" Amy is stunned. "He said that there were 'bomb-blasts!'"

"-Tinitus" Another quick button press deadens the screen. "Our friend here is the only one left. His view of this 'war' must be a little cloudy, at least." Realising that my outburst is unwelcome, I'm soon brushing Amy's nose with my fingertip. "I'm sorry, I had hoped we'd find somewhere a little less hectic to lick our

50

wounds..." I search out my bifocals from a jacket pocket.

Amy nods, she has sat on the table and pulls her knees up to her chin. The soldier has come too, and his brown eyes offer her grateful thanks: it must be so odd for him; we must appear as misfits carving out an existence on a world he knows as Derva Six.

"I assume you had some sort of plan you were working out?" He nods: it had been a simple strategy, lost in the intricate detail of the paperwork, the various maps and the weaponry: they formed the plan so long ago and the deafening blasts have he feels, exploded it from his memory.

Almost.

"Why are you here? Is it to help me, gain victory, over the Derva?"

"-To end the Dervan War?"; suddenly, I'm unsure. "Yes..." I say at last.

He staggers over to the map of the battleground. Hencho's lovingly featured masterpiece, marked out with red flags, which
now must symbolise Hencho's own blood..

"Ah, seems your Commander-"

"-Jeffries..."

"-Jeffries, yes. Seems to have had a thing about tactical withdrawals..."

"The plan had some basic deficiencies..." He begins to explain: if we have been sent to help fight the war on Derva, there are some things we should know.

"Of course!" My spectacles shift down to the edge of his nose. "Your loving commander devised a weapon so efficient nobody could live to benefit from it. He's only done one decent thing in this war man, got himself wiped out before he could devise you all out of existence!"

The soldier tires of my lack of respect for the dead. Amy agrees with him. "-I meant in numbers, I am the only one left, at least in any condition to fight..."

Amy clambers over, studying the map: and then the soldier - with equal distaste."You're not in any condition to fight!"He studies her quizzically: she is strong, but does she have the stamina to end this war? The Martakian race, of which Amy is one border of

51

pacifism; however their strength lies in reproduction.

"-And neither could you, negotiate..." I summarise bleakly.

"A few well-intentioned grunts and the shaking of fists, may be fine for basic communication and foreplay..." Amy considers.

"You've met them before?" I gasp.

"No," Amy gets all defensive."My knowledge is gleaned from our records..."Amy taps her temples with each thumb.

"Communicate with the Derva never!" The soldier's eyes burn from betrayal."They would kill me first."

"Cliched nonsense!" I turn on him, "In some respects the Derva are just like you. Only, not as pig-headedly stubborn!"

"Andrew, if you have a peaceful solution to any of this me and the pig-head would love you to enlighten us, perhaps even show us..." She suggests coyly.

"You want me to negotiate with -?"

"-I'm sure that by morning you'll reach the point where you're both grunting the same language..."

***

So it is that I set off with some provisions from the suitcase; a torn white sheet; some minor tools; and the crudest of deactivation kits; also, the Geographic Analyser - should I find the Derva I want to know its mood.

"Oh dear..." At first, I don't find the Derva I've found someone the records will name Hencho: although he's unidentifiable, his face is decomposing before me, under a torrent of insects. I often wonder why Amy always sends me on reconnaissance, but it may be because of my tepid bargaining skills. All I have to do is follow the path away from the lava, and that should be easy: if my toes begin to melt, I'll know I'm in trouble.

Derva Six has changed so much since last time: the locals have enhanced their planting skills: moving away from bleak barren desserts: of use only to low budget sci-fi movies and harvesting Cardilla Herb. The results are all around; self planted wild bushes are singing in this heat. Jeffries and his army have tipped the balance: 'The Cardilla Herb,' once the perfect resource, in this crumbled blackened form in my palm and soon coating my tongue - it tastes vile.

Ah, I've arrived. This is a superior looking dome, barely dented and set deep in vegetation. I look down at my few negotiation devices; hopefully, I'm not about to be heat detected. War is not the place for old men: eccentric warmonger Commanders excepted. Talking peace with the Derva can apparently be like having ingrowing toenails removed, without a knock on the head.... Wait they've seen me: it has clammy brown skin and moves in a staggering motion. The face is strange in its strangest form: deep set, guarded and a khaki shade to its ears - almost as if our Derva 'friend' were wearing a ma..sk...

"Ah, yes of course..."; He's seen me: this is the time to get up and move slowly forwards. We meet each other's eyes. "I'd like to talk to you about a god..." I say.

The Derva have changed: they no longer speak coherently and their movements are cumbersome; they have no difficulty in allowing a potential aggressor into their domain: I say, 'they' my biggest surprise is that only one, remains, okay, the map on the wall showing a battle plan y almost identical, to the Commander's one at the base was my biggest surprise - it seems Jeffries was a double agent. I study the Derva's wooden box in the corner of the room...

***

Having gained entry and left leaflets, I settle into a spiel about how democracy works. By the early hours, I've employed my crude bomb deactivating device, Rankonian wine - it works a dream but for one small fact: The Derva are so docile at war that in an alcoholic daze they actually become more alert.

"Let me show you how to make the flag..."; I pull all the oddments from my bag.   The Derva focusses on the many components placed across his floor of this tiny wooden shack. "You want an end to this war, yes?" He doesn't say it: but it's obvious that is its wish. So, I'm teaching him to wave the flag. "If you want peace, you, use this, understand?" It could be that horrible alien glint in his eye: yet at that point I'm glad I defused his bomb and that his box now only contains the phrasebook: I have disarmed our aggressor...

"Peace? He did it?" The Derva smirks at me.

"The soldier from the other side arranged this? Yes, he's tired of fighting and battle worn!"

"You, want peace too?"

"Yes. One day. Commander, he said: 'One day'." He glares at me honestly, "Now, I want, piece, too!" Well this has gone well, shrewd negotiation with a supposed savage, they're even dressed the same: he has number '126' emblazoned on his breast.

"Tomorrow at first light, you can have peace tomorrow..." I promise him.

"He will want, piece too?" The Derva lifts the flag. "Weapons?" He grimaces.

"-No weapons. No." I steady my hand on his shoulder. "Just want peace, too." And he is calmed: that is that, the Derva posed no threat to me - other than the unfamiliar odour; some things really can be solved with pleasant conversation: Satisfied, I return to base...

"It's keen to negotiate?" The soldier is sceptical upon my return, and Amy, is more so than he.

"Jeffries, was a double agent, wanted to be on the winning side?" "Yes," I look upwards, "even so, in the strictest of forums, you can't have a winning side when everyone's internal organs' kiss the sky!" Amy reasons that in war, logic seldom comes into it.

Our route will deviate slightly from my earlier path; the remains of Hencho belong to the more scenic route. They would be bad for morale, and less ideally we will cross, what our incapacitated friend has come to know as a forest of bombs. Luckily, our soldier counters that one direct hit from the Derva would have bought the dome roof down upon him: and dying on a field of battle is better than being crushed, like a shrew behind a refrigerator - it is my experience that descendants of the human have gained increasingly fertile and thoroughly unpleasant terms of metaphor, throughout time; I was thinking that in fact a sneeze from a passing dung fly would have the same result: what is wrong with that? It saves the thoughts of crushed furry rodent: but what can one expect, from a being who describes himself as meccano? Amy places down his stretcher in the dry, crumbly mud.

"Can I ask how you were injured?" The soldier wants to know: I view him impatiently, scoffing at his nerve in letting Amy recall such an horrific ordeal.

"My friend had a tribulation with a crossbow."

He watches Amy distantly. "'Cross-bow'?" He has not heard the word before.

"I, myself, was mentally-scarred, myself in a world, where perception is graded by life experience." I'm hissing through my teeth but he doesn't care: just nods: and says: 'I seem the sort that would be.'

Amy has gone on ahead but soon retreats back towards us. She has seen something. "There's a big red patch, blood..." She announces.

"Hencho," the soldier coughs, bringing up some more of his own, on my shirt: the jacket's already gelled around his rotting carcass.

"Why don't you go and bleed over someone else?" I glare back.

Amy comes between us and pats the soldier's arm, noting my fiery expression."Go easy on him Andrew..."; *"Go easy?!": I've covered more ground; been gobbed on; and followed two rivers of lava to get him out of his shell.*

"So there were how many Derva, when the war began?" Amy asks him, as I stroll distantly ahead. When I look back, her eyes are shining in acquaintance.

"-And what do they want?" I wonder.

"The planet!?" The soldier speculates: He doesn't know: how typical of his species to be at war with a race when he doesn't even know what's the true agenda.

"How, boring!" Amy objects.

"-All planets are boring! Just lumps of rock in space that got big ideas above their station!" I'm striding ahead, so angry with why I've come to be on this wretched... "So, they infested themselves with the biggest, whinger,"

"-Andrew!" Amy grabs my arm and pulls me roughly back. "Watch your step..." She cautions, circling the area with the analyser. "It's safe!"

"-I know it's safe!" The soldier does not believe us."There are no bombs here," I tap the wood on his tightly grasped container. "Other than the ones you have in your little boxes..."

"Something here though..."Amy is pulling loose vegetation away; our soldier friend is staggered."A rough-terrain vehicle!" Amy beams, smiling at him.

He staggers backwards muttering, 'Booby trapped!' Some people will never take advantage of providence: and it's exactly where I was promised it would be...

"You are, the Derva?" He glowers at her but especially at me." Have I been betrayed?"; For someone left to die in his own mess; this soldier has nothing but contempt for his guardian angels.

"No, the analyser," my lecture begins as I snatch the device from Amy. "The device picks up and transmits brainwaves." He can sense nervousness in my words.

"Well, Amy's the specialist."; He doesn't get it: in the crudest of forms I expect him to believe that it is the spirit of Hencho that guided us here?

"You speak of sorcery?" His turn to scoff. "The girl is bewitched".

"'Bewitched'?"

"Ninety's super-group or charming, if repetitive American Sitcom," Amy reads from the analyser and shrugs. "'Enchanted. In love...gormless," she selects another word from the memory. "Charmed, who's Shannen Doherty? " Amy frowns; the analyser's on the blink again: hopefully, he'll believe me; I'm trying to show that we can be trusted but I must have one of those faces, I'm afraid.

"No matter, there is no-one else."

Amy observes him sympathetically. "You have little hope or

leaving here alive, without us."; Maybe I would not have stated that so explicitly: timidly he boards the vehicle: his face shows that he knows that Amy is right.

The buggy gleams: it must have belonged to the Derva; the mechanisms shine and the displays are soon illuminated. Then, Amy shows she is indeed, 'the specialist'. We move quickly over the dry terrain. She controls the vehicle like a patient lover, guiding first with gentle prods, then violently lurching to gain dominance over the sickly motor functions; finally a steadied fist shows that she's in control.

"She still so reminds me of my Cardilla..." The soldier smiles at me as tears well up in his eyes. To a soldier not used to being so densely within this landscape, we must appear detached, cold: to others I often feel we resemble sightseers. He trembles. His colleagues line the route ahead, splattered like gull droppings haphazardly where they fell: we seem to just accept it.

On another world we saw humans herded to incinerators: grown men attempting a lottery of life and balking at the consequences - death; no consequence to us. On Notorious, an alien species found it enjoyed watching people being murdered: so it mutated to torture without question for eternity: it fractured time: wiping out the Earth, as if it were an oily finger stain on a soon to be bleached display case...

"So, am I, alone?" The soldier interrupts my wandering muse, with his question. Amy looks back and wipes a tear from his eye, sucking the salt on her fingers: I wish she wouldn't do that.

"Being alone is just a state of mind, gives you time to think.."

The trouble is, she doesn't think! Oh wild, compassionate, Martakian Parasite: don't tell a lonely man that being alone allows time to think; would you tell a dying man that he needed time to die? Come to think of it - she probably would. We lurch: the display on Amy's analyser, glows red, she glares at me and in that split second our buggy swerves.

Amy snatches the control stick but it seems bulky and awkward, she fights heroically: unfortunately, we strayed into a lava pool and the tyres couldn't take it - they burst. The planet surface cracks, the

57

buggy lurches sideways: we twist and lurch and topple out. Our buggy explodes as it's sucked into the planets' frothy nothingness.

"It appears we have no choice..." Amy considers bleakly.

The soldier panics and squeezes the box to him. "To cross this desert on foot must be sheer craziness, "; yet, with neither of us reacting to his panic, he bemoans that he went mad some days ago and is now the only one sane enough to realise this. "We are in a battle-zone!" The soldier laments, "Any moment we will be blown to fragments."; If he doesn't stop whining, I'm going to dunk him in a bloody lava pool nose first; besides his imagery is wrong in a battle-zone, one is usually shot to fragments or blown to pieces - he whinges far too much for a reliable narrator.

"-Assuming, the secret weapon doesn't kill us first." Amy grabs the box from the soldier's clasp. He explains that he never even knew he had it, just clung on: strange what men cling to in troubled times...

"So, unless, I'm very much mistaken..."

"-That's, it?" Amy considers it quizzically then, follows my finger to the dome. "It's barely dented," she glares back at me and then to the soldier and the dome. "It's like. They're not, very efficient, shots are they?"The soldier is unimpressed. He counters that Jeffries explained the dome had been hit and...

"Hencho wouldn't lie!" He had confirmed their Commander's story.

"-That's what it was, a story!" The soldier glares at me as if I had just sworn. "How long were you part of this squadron, how-come, the battle map doesn't have any input from you?"

"I don't know what you mean..." He replies.

"No?" So I grab his tunic: I can show him the number. "Look at this; One-two-One." I stab at the numerals on his jacket with my finger. "You are the Derva, and the Derva is you!"

"The same squadron," Amy frowns, "How can that be?"

"They were on a training exercise!"

Amy despairs, "I hope you can rationalise that, Andrew..." She states frostily. The soldier is waiting to pounce. "They killed my

Cardilla," he bemoans. "We would have had a family together!"

I tug a leaf from the nearby bush and hurl it into his face. "Your Cardilla!" I announce savagely, "This is, 'Your Cardilla'... The rest is all a drug-induced fantasy. Cardilla is a smoked herb created by a half-hearted war game!"

"No!"

"They left you and a friend in the forest, a scenario to follow. They wanted, to see how you reacted..."

"No way,"

"Yes, the Derva is part of your squadron,";Amy cannot believe me; She says I've been fed wrong information, got it wrong somehow:"-What about the bodies?" She asks, growling at me as I hold her back.

"Even a War game can become dangerous: earthquakes? Lava? They couldn't get them out: Jeffries, tripped out. So they abandoned them here...."

"-And-you-know-this-how?"

"-Doesn't matter, the Derva wants peace Amy, he told me himself..."

Amy pauses to think. "You better, be right about this Andrew..." The soldier slowly approaches the door of the dome - and then the door opens...

"Open the box..." My voice carries across the blood arena. The soldier looks into the box despairingly. He steps back."Wave your flag!" I call to him.

"You have disarmed the Derva?" He ponders.

"Yes," Amy looks back at me: she isn't sure.

"Yes. The bomb's defused, the Commander just went mad never got to finish the exercise."

"That's alright then," the soldier ventures in...

***

Long moments have passed, before, finally we hear a blood freezing scream.

"Wrong Andrew. You got it wrong!" Amy pushes me away as she sprints towards the door...

"He, dead," The Derva greets us: something was lost in translation I fear."I have, piece now!"; My eye's focus on our soldier's pierced stomach pierced by the sharpened end of our white flag: and the 'peace' that the Derva has is the head of his enemy: and I know that I have failed...

***

Amy walked slowly out, I didn't stop her, just reached for the dusty phrasebook, something had been lost in translation? Only my self-respect.

After a moment, I removed the white-flag: and imagined the Derva sharpening the end; eager for the kill and enhancing his blood lust with how the flag-cloth would smear with his enemies' blood. Then, I spent long moments examining the tip, now stained - with the blood of peace....

***

"Andrew?" He stopped me in the corridor; Amy was being patched up in the Medi-wing, me? I just needed a breather.

"Do I know you?" He doesn't seem familiar: but after transfer some people never settle in your memory, they just fidget there.

"You will," he says, and I know that he is right. "You can see why the history books say the War on Derva never happened?"

"Oh yes, it's been written down as the longest 'trip' in history: but I never believe the history books..."

"All of the evidence corroborates with the official version of events?"

"It will now. He might have recognised me, you know?"

"That would have been tricky, not as big an embarrassment as what really happened."

"-A phoney-war, on a, dead world? I take your point: an environmental disaster that conveniently wipes out a rogue commander and his green troops in a one day training exercise..."

"I couldn't possibly comment..."

"-An embarrassment though: the climate evolves; yet the war continues: throughout time. What was it? Time acceleration experiment? Evolution developing, a race evolving to be forever at war with itself..."

"Your explanation for the herb was inspired..."

"-Best-thing I, could think of at the time, 'Cardilla Herb': don't-ever, expect me to lie for you again."

He smiles, patting his file. "Oh, we won't, Andrew. How else could we expect a noted humanitarian of Amy's calibre to help bring events to a close? You have seen the records and Amy has verified them?" He ponders for a moment. "I understand your Assistant, is still not convinced?"

"Leaving transportation was sloppy. We led that man to his death and she wants to know, why?"

"An unresolved conflict: now that no trace remains of the unfortunate little hiccup. If it helps you to sleep at night remember, they might have made peace..."

"-On a dying world?" My head shakes, almost of its own accord. "Just pawns in your very nasty little game weren't we?" I despair. 'However you are wrong, the soldier, he left.. diaries: very detailed diaries. Amy insists they be printed up for, 'historical' purposes..."

"-A maverick soldier reaching his finest hour? We have no objection."

"So, that's agreed then, will you need to, censor them before they go to public records?"

He doesn't feel that will be necessary: I will print them out when I have finished translating them: but the astonishing thing about them is how they go well beyond our soldier friend's death and tell exactly what occurred on Derva. They will be on restricted access for hundreds of years, save for just a few influential historians: and though I say it myself, those historical documents from the computer files of Derva?

Let's just say that I consider them among my finest works...

Notes : Fantasy and Science Fiction remain a great playground for the imagination – and even some UK Women's Magazines' are realising that a little fantasy can be a good thing..

Four O' Clock shadow was offered to some darker American markets, including Flesh and Blood, as "FORESHADOW", for its appearance here, I've made some minor changes for tone – sometimes ,it's just the title that seems wrong – back in 2000 I was walking past a hairdressing salon and I saw the notice that Lucy had a baby boy – I took it as possible inspiration – when the story was ready – I took inspiration from the story itself; I realised that "Sometimes, you have to go back.."

Four O' Clock Shadow

He didn't draw attention to himself at first; just a man seated in a yellow cab, blending into the kerb-side: it was only as my tracking device fidgeted in my palm that I knew he'd outstayed his allotted time.

"Excuse me," I'm soon tapping on his front window screen, and he's hunching his shoulders. "Are you broken down?" He's sat in there wearing a mack. No response, is he ignoring me? Or can't he hear me? Through the opening window I scan his eardrums - he grabs at my arm: his eyes are fixed, it's like he can't really see me. I pull violently away.

He scowls back at me.

"I thought you needed help to move on."He pats the passenger seat and opens the door: edgily, I join him.

"Can, you hear?" He asks me, still scowling.

"Yes," I glare back: yes I can although his words are crackly and his focus, remains hazy.

He nods sadly, "I feel so sorry for you," he replies, "you miss so much."

"I Said, 'Yes', I can."

"I know." He flusters. "I'm just resting," he pauses, "I have a lot on my mind." ; And I know there's going to be no discussion: he just has that kind of face, deep-set and intent. His eyes, they'd boss you around.

"You're going on a journey?"

"I haven't decided where I want to go yet." He flicks a page of his newspaper.

"You can't stay here. You'll have to move on."

"How do you know that?" He catches my eye before rubbing his sleeve over his nose."This might be 'my place': I might be, really happy here."

"How long have you been here?"

"Time is relative," he pulls a hairy wrist into his gaze. "I

63

arrived at four O' clock. I've been watching humanity playing on the swings."

"You'll have to move on." I try and reason, searching for my book of tickets.

"Why? What's it to you?"

"-That's my job," my back pocket is also empty. "Telling 'others' when it's time to move-on."

"Goodness," he scoffs, "aren't we being Politically Correct?" He glares back at me. "'Ghost' is the name you're looking for."

"You're not a ghost," I check the latest readings, "not really. You didn't develop from an awakening of the past; affect everything around you, hanging around like the five o'clock shadow on my chin. A nuisance, and you'll have to move on."

"I've already said that I've been here since four o' clock."

"-You're a four o' clock shadow then: it makes no difference to me...""So easy for you isn't it?" He snaps back at me

"What do you mean?"He rubs at his hat and places the newspaper on the dashboard. "I've been affected by what I've seen here: kids in the playground." He points across the road in front of us: to the 'safe' area with the climbing frames, slides and woodchips."Soon be playing with guns; knifing each other; smoking dope, for real." He rubs at his eyes. "It's affecting me."

"So you're a ghost haunted by what's yet to come. "-I thought we'd agreed, I wasn't a ghost?!"

"-That's what they'd understand you as," I reason. "Humans can't grab big concepts: it'll make their heads ache. "So what am I, to you, I mean?"

"I've already told you: you're a shadow...a four O'clock shadow, knowing all things, yet haunted by yourself!" I puzzle over my scanner readings, "-Your inability to do anything about them..." He watches me as my head shakes in confusion.

"-You mean, a ghost that haunts himself?" This seems to delight him.

I hold his arm firmly, "-And, I'm here to tell you that you must move on."

He nods, pointing over across the street. "See that girl?"; I don't not at first - there are so many of them: of the female gender, "Over there?" Then I do; there's a girl smiling with her friends by the school gates - she has long bunched dark hair, and, as he points out: the cutest smile.

"Yes..." I say.

"-She's going to die,"

I become agitated.

"-Not yet!" He tries to assure me. "In two days time, only she won't just 'die' - one of their kind: he ends it for her, they'll find her body in the - "

"-I don't want to know!"

"No," he pity's me, "you don't - do you? They'll find her in their playground strangled," he shows his hands. "Murdered: they'll never solve the case, this will devastate her family," he shakes his head. "They'll be more casualties..."

"-Stop it!" I growl, "I said, 'I don't want to know!'"

"Imagine," he sighs glumly. "The playground across the road, all human life is slowly dying: you could go to her: tell her to wait back after school."

"-I can't do tha-"

"-You, 'won't' do that - and you call me a shadow?!"

"-What does that mean?"

"At the very least I have a mandate: humanity assumes there's a presence watching over them; guiding their kids; their family; their siblings." He snorts, "What-are-you?"

"-I don't know what you mean..."

"I tell you things will happen: yet you choose not to act," he sighs, "just sit there with your rule book telling me to 'move on'."

"Humanity can't cope with you," I explain, "-It's rolling itself into the perfect little ball; preparing for the worst - yet expecting the best because that's humanity: if you told them everything that was to happen - they'd never leave their beds in the morning..."

"-Can't they decide what they want to hear?"

"-Not from you, you're a shadow..."

"I'm just watching, I'm not scaring them; they're scaring me," he rubs sadly at his eyes. "I want to move on: but I'm haunted..."

"-It, affects me-too!" I confess: it's like all my realisations have come from this, figment, this, between-worlde.

65

"-It, does?" He gasps.

"The horror of it all: the murders; the suicides; the accidents - the apathy. You become desensitised: because you can't dwell on it or you'd never move on. It becomes addictive."

"-Humanity, addictive?"

"Yes!" I admit triumphantly: I couldn't do my job if I didn't keep that fact - at the very least, somewhere in my mind.

"So," he stares back at me, "'You' have to move-on - before it starts to affect 'you'?" He smiles.

"I've never had that problem," I assure myself and him simultaneously. "I only have to watch for a little while..."

"-And, I only want to watch for a little while!"

"How long have you, been observing them?"

He glances at his watch. "You, know?" He sighs, picking up the newspaper from the dashboard.

"-Since, four o'clock?" I repeat, "-This, afternoon?"

"-All afternoons! But you're right: It'll soon be my time to move on."

"Five more minutes won't hurt!" I reply reasonably. "I said to my assistant: 'See him? He's a drifter: Parked in

his cab, watching the time go by: have to get him to move on.'"

"-But, five more minutes won't hurt!"

"-That's right!" I check my scanner and fold my arms cheerily, "What's another five minutes?" I nod.

"-It's not the easiest job in the world," he sighs: trying to find the sports pages.

"You, haunt people," I frown, "They, haunt you..."

"That's what I said, yes..."

"Then, it's not a job at-all: it's a vocation!" I point out matter of factually.

"-But, I don't enjoy doing it..."

"Then, it's a job!" I concur

"How long have you been doing your job?"

"-Asking others to, move-on?"

He nods..

"-A long time," I lament. "You're the stubbornest one I've met. Usually, I just give 'em a push in the right direction!"

"-It, sounds like a very boring job," he considers, "have you considered changing it?"

"I can't do that..."

"-Not even for five minutes?" He's puzzled, and soon he's tapping his fingers on the dashboard. "What kind of a job is it where you're not even off duty for that long?"

I'm adamant: this position is the whole essence of my physical being - my reason for existing; but he doesn't understand, doesn't want to understand.

"I can help you to break your contract - that way you'd find a job with better prospects.

"-Your five minutes is up!" He glares at me: and I'm very, very angry.

"Just five more minutes," He asks reasonably. ' -To read my paper?!" He sounds confident, tries to explain that he can show me a new side to myself - one unfettered by the grip of the body: I'd be free to negotiate my own terms.

"I said, 'Your five minutes is up! You'll have to move-on!"

"-Now?"

I look down at my feet then back up at him, his face a dignified acceptance of my request.

"-I'm, sorry..."

"So am I." He says: and with that, he brings a taste of his world to mine, as he lunges forward, then I, black out with my head dropping onto the dashboard...

*

When I awake, a figure in a mack, is leering over me

"I'm sorry sir, but you'll have to move-on!"

"No," I'm most insistent: scrambling through my pockets for the tracer for the rule-book: for any sign of authority. "You're the one who has to move-on," I fumble lamely in my coat

"I'm afraid. I just did!" He shows me "our" rule-book through the car window, disapprovingly: as my heart goes rocky-cold.

Hard Times on Seferon Black

JOURNAL OF BELONIA STEVENS: DAY ONE

My father was a grade one "Brain-Physch" from the "outer galaxies". He met my mother on a Medicentre ward while on his lunchbreak. How they "fell in love", I do not know: mum always said he got into her head somehow.

Anyway, they made me and constructed a home in a luxury living bay on Seferon Green, an isolate's world: only professionals, their kids and their cleaners lived there; mum thought I'd grow up an isolate, so dad would take me to work with him at a Medicentre on Seferon Grey.

Squeamish, I know: but by the age of twelve I'd have my brain augmented with the latest fad in music, in their mistaken belief that it would stimulate me to a higher level. Dad was by then a highly skilled mind surgeon for Tapestry Technologies. He had arrived! With this container of coloured cubes he'd just attach to a computer.

The "subject" would talk through their mental anguish: it was often fascinating how daddy could just control them with the cubes. All I wanted to do was watch as some poor waif opened their perceptions, relieved of the burden that was their past. Sometimes, I would sit by daddy's side as the subject was "sleeping" and hear them murmuring: by that point they were usually docile and wet...

One day, I learned that father would not be taking me again: some "expert" had decided to remove the human factor from brain psych., the cubes of which father had been so all embracing, would be robbing him of his job; Brain Psych was the gentle way to massage the mind. Some "whizz" in research had found a way to hasten the process; They'd remove one cube, outlaw it, and with that dad would become, in his terms, "a mind rapist..."; The new cubes could help them all; With the cubes you could now do more than suck the undesirable qualities from the mind; Gentle questioning, hypnotism and logic would be superseded.

The population would be mapped out as a mass of radical chemicals that they could dissect at will, to allow only the base elements of human function...

'Belonia...' My father would say to me and I'd search out, the outline of his skull against the top of the ceiling, 'a worker needs only one attribute...'; He'd show me the only cube they no longer permitted him to use...

His small grey box of cubes sat idly for many years after that. This was a pride thing with him, also a respect and a care for his patients. His permits and certificates went out of phase - then evaporated, they dated quickly. Father got himself an administrative position - they say he died getting up for his ration break; his body wasn't used to moving.

Although I made it my business to follow on from my father's work, I didn't get on well with "Mind-Phase" the new name for "Brain-phych"; So when my apprenticeship came up, I opted for the only area where they still sanctioned manipulation cubes - processing centres - used for work manipulation.

In time, I got the kind of work my father would have envied - face to face contact; Talking resting future employees through their "wish-lists" to match with their prospects of employment; That was around the time my blaster first became locked on Grendell Adams...

Initially, I liked him, the sort of person my father would have loved to psychoanalyse: a rough man with much facial hair, an unkempt scruffy bearded man with a relaxed view of personal hygiene. He called me a "pushy little Android," he was right - if Grendell and I had lived together we'd have incurred my father's greatest rage...

It was obvious from the start that Grendell would be a challenge. He had lived most of his life on Seferon blue, an appalling world of bare forests and stagnant populations. There was nothing on the blue planet but Medicentres and funeral homes. Grendell had carved a living as a idealist; an artist; a reporter and a Freelancer. He sent stories to the zones: Children's stories and romantic fiction along with the dead language, once known as Sci-Fi.

Grendell had friends that could harvest this talent, yet his skills were becoming dated and work drained away following the terrible plagues and the burning of the zones.

In the summer of his thirtieth year, we decided that Grendell should see an advisor. He had made piddling efforts into updating his computer skills and could even send proposals via telekinesis. Writing remained his first love though, and he was certainly determined.

Grendell had several letters from disgruntled editors, circulars in the main; it seemed he just hadn't got the hint. Oh, and he had "contacts in the media". Yet, he had abandoned his art to follow the requirements of his work-finding agreement.

How weak it seems now, but I did not wish to crush his spirit. Grendell was ill, an unstable digestive disorder, which had developed from a lifetime of employment in the seasonal outposts. Although he had a memorable fragrance and a relaxed mode of dress, we sat talking for a long five minutes. I felt that socialisation, and more up to date training regimes would help. Positions were sometimes available within the corporation, and I felt certain they would find him suitable areas for his talent. With my contacts, I arranged that he should see about the many wider options attainable.

Grendell was keen, tracking employment was an expensive pursuit and he knew that writing came from his soul and he could adapt it into his working day. He would go to the Processing Centre for reallocation...

My name is Grendell, I was a poet a writer that was my designation.

I am laying here an absolute mess; they were fine at first, offering me beverages; guiding me you might say: Then I learned the truth.

The Corporation wants me for manual labour on Seferon Black.

They need "willing volunteers" for their mining work, or I can try my luck at a seasonal outpost as a bingo caller.

Miserable. That is how I feel; I could have taken a training course in android technologies, or updated my language skills at a Learning Curve.

Betrayed, I feel betrayed: They promised to mould me into an administrative position. I know administration, the smell of paper or the feel of compact disks.

I am a husk: now, they want me to forget my past, to widen my scope, not a man of culture but a shell: a shell that has not shaved, a sweaty stinking shell of burned out ambition.

It seems obvious to me now: They have re-programmed me: I know how they did it,

"Writing is a hobby" for "children" you have to be realistic. You have defrauded your local Employment bureau."

'Writing is a hobby!' That is what really hurts: I never felt I had given anything less than my best. I payed for the computer course myself, from my allowances, and as I sit there editing my life, retyping it: They are just options on a screen.

"Writing is a hobby. You defrauded us."

Grendell Adams is a con man to be treated as cannon fodder for the bloody agency! They have destroyed me, if they don't let me write, I am nothing! Just a number on a computer screen.

I feel sick. I have layed in this darkened room hearing how they mock me, how they will wake me up to the real world.

'This is my world!'

They envision a world of monitor screens and pin numbers, RSI and tender-back chairs. I was never a monitor slave on Sefron Blue; I used to go walking, with a voice-recorder or my laptop: I control *the terminal: it does not control me; Only the un-contracted would allow themselves to be controlled by their machines, it was in my jousts with "Thesaurus" and "Grammar Checker" that I learned to overcome.*

They said that "Though there are many areas of the brain more finely mapped than a woman's cleavage," there was no way "to remove pig-ignorance, save for the mere automaton." I think: therefore, I present a challenge.

That paragraph is wordy, I know it is wordy and if you give me a chance...I shall correct it.

I know what has happened. At nine this morning, I crashed, I was speaking cliche, cliche! ; Though I hold my head in my hands "Macaliister-esque": like the little boy left home alone by the parables of motion theatres: what does that word mean? It was in an old dictionary and it suited the scene, alright?

'But what does it mean?'

I don't know!

I felt the descent of my muse: it died an agonisingly painful death, inside my head.

'That's original...'

Must: I will hold it together.

The tenders flowers of autumn prose.

The harsh-winter acid tongue.

Of someone who has lost his soul.

The reams of paper; the stacks of disks; and the dreams of success; all gone.

Well, I will not be re-programmed. I am not a number: I am a freelance writer! Belonia, my advisor did not promise riches: but she has betrayed me. I am not going to bend to their will, ever!

'You are making it difficult for yourself Grendell!'

That is right. I am a long way from home, even in super-drive and what they call an isolate; a being that has removed them-self, to pursue my own ambitions: you will not have me, Corporation.

Now, I can hear the voices: They are starting to pound upon my door....

FROM THE JOURNAL OF BELONIA STEVENS: DAY FOUR

Processing did not go well, Grendell is tall and imposing, and while he was keen to seek employment and search for the vacancies as agreed, something did not click. The corporation let me know of the problem almost from the first day.

My agreement with Grendell and the way we had handled him, and nourished his 'artistic flare.' (I have never heard artistic sound so like a swearword) had damaged his future prospects. Corporation had a degrading manner of control, which I have not fully

realised. Our agreement was just a guide; Grendell would go through reprogramming to try to starve this spirit out.

Naturally, I took the first cruiser that I could get to Sefron Blue...

I respect his need to express himself; trapped as he is in that heavy frame. Against the blue misty oceans of Sefron Blue, as this, mode of transport, this spacious fragile freighter clunks into power-drive, I could get romantically expressive and breed an economically healthy imagination: I think we all could...

From the Journal of Grendell Adams: date unknown

Have you seen me? Have you seen, me? My beard is, wisps, my head is hot, my back is stooping: I have typed the formula; it was just like letters only, it was not the poetry of words but the squeak of

73

decimal: it is all part of my scam to play along; let them think they have me...

I shall never wear the regulation uniform of Sefron Black, it is bright red, pure Will Robinson you might say: clothes should express character, they should smell of wool and cotton, not the inside of a squeaky zip.

I shall never bend to their will; The ink may be dry in the printer, but if the corporation asks: I shall tell them about myself - not present myself as a list to be gasped at, sidelined and binned.

I shall resist all efforts to brainwash me...
Some efforts to...
A few efforts to...
I am nothing...

FROM THE JOURNAL OF BELONIA STEVENS: DAY FIVE

'I shall deal with this gentleman.' The room is dark as I step across and pull up the covers.

'This isn't necessary. I'm not going to be seduced!' Grendell warns me and seems firm set in his ways; Fortunately, I have many other means at my disposal and I reach across to his forehead as I consider how best to treat him. Where he has rested his head on the pillow, it is hot and his hair has become matted. 'I'm not a number. I'm a freelance writer.'

'Of course you are,'; I can see how his mind is weeping in the confusion.'Why don't you tell me about it?' I sit beside his bed and we talk, finally I know what I must do; The cube terminal displays a gruesome collection of horrors, from "obedience" to "loyalty", I stare across at Grendell, recalling another time, grasping the cube...

I like to see the subject twist; dad would be able slowly to phase in the alteration over time and gently begin "the resting time." However, I might lose my Grendell and with him, my bonus. I open my briefcase and hold the purple cube so that it catches the light in his eyes.

'Let him have all these qualities..., '; I can recall dad in mid-lecture 'and one more besides...'; The cube goes into the slot, as it should have all along...

FROM AN UNPUBLISHED WORK BY GRENDELL ADAMS

'Why don't you tell me about it?' She kisses my cheek and then I know that very soon we will know everything about each other: there is no pretence, I am Grendell Adams and she desires me as richly as she would, a water-hole in a tropical haven. Soon, we are naked and when we find contentment; I will nourish her
soul with my poetry... and we will reveal everything about each other; I shall have control of her always...

***

Grendell looks so smart in his red overalls. We didn't do anything but talk, no matter what he says in his diaries, I know he will say something because he was undressing me with his eyes. The uniform does not suit him. The label is rubbing against his neck. They glare at me as I take Grendell's hand, I am going to be considered a traitor.

'What glorious offer have you brokered?' They explain that they have a contract with this unfortunate, they pay him credits and want only his stamina and muscle to seek those realistic areas of employment.

'Can, Grendell, 'the brain' be persuaded, might he willingly go to the selection process at the Gateway?'

'You'd allow him to go back and search unrealistic avenues on the outer planets? You are weak, Belonia...' As they speak, Grendell brushes himself down and begins lumbering of his own accord towards hatchway one, manual labour.

'What did you agree, Belonia?'
'How can you control such a determined spirit?'
'No deals, gentlemen, Grendell is willing to fulfil his contracted terms.' ;He has bowed to the inevitable: I gave Grendell my word

that we would realise his full potential and I must see that is so. Being a writer on Sefron Black will take every ounce of his being, and I must ensure that he never fulfills that; He will develop new potential as "a lumbering, rock-breaking, chipped-handed, oaf".

The aggression, he will need shall come from the energy of frustration; of a fantasy, unfulfilled - that failure will be invaluable to us - yes I intend him to live up to his full potential and, I realise, with a certain degree of pride, that I have full-filled my potential too; I have gained something their crude 'skill

absorbing' methods could not: by returning to Grendell a quality upon which my father and I insist.

'Did you burn his mind?'

'No, I simply gave him back one basic attribute...'

'What have you, given him, back?'; A final wave, a cheeky grin and my Grendell 's gone forever behind the shutters of adversity.

'I gave him back his right to dream, gentleman. I gave him back his right to dream...'.   © **2002**

notes :If you've ever tried to stay writing while under the scrutiny of the job centre you'll have some sympathy with this; a world where you're not allowed to be creative – can you even imagine living in such a world? As to whether it's based on real events...I couldn't possibly comment...

Lucy Had a Baby Girl

'Francessca,' he's shaking his head. 'What do you look like?' He despairs, 'What will Lucy think?'

'She's, busy!' I stare ahead.

He rubs at his chin. 'Just remember, don't stay too long..' He advises me, 'It'll be dangerous...'

'I might run into the owner!'

'Don't even joke about that!' He sniggers, studying me through the early morning murk. 'You'll do!' He smiles. 'Have you got the folder?'

I nod, indicating the shopping bag.

'-And your umbrella?' He looks up at the sky and hands me the wrapped umbrella – which I place in my pocket.

'What if she get's suspicious?'

'Then finish it, get out of there..' He pulls me back to him. 'Now, you're certain about this escape route?'

'Yes!' I roll my eyes. 'I've been here before, remember?'

'Top of the stairs and turn right?' He checks for the seventeenth time that day. 'I'll cover for you..'

'Okay..'

Looking back, he pulls a stray strand of hair out of my eyes. 'Now remember why we're doing this..' He breathes out.

'-For the, both of us?'

He nods

***

'I saw the sign in the window,' I said.

'Oh, yes.' Marion is brushing up the stray strands of hair from the chequered floor; I say "Marion", she might have borrowed the apron; although it fitted like a glove – but I doubt many gloves would be as large and homely. She's clutching a piece of green card with the words "ROOM TO LET" scrawled on it. 'Did you park

77

your motorbike around the side?" She smiles.

'My, motorbike?" I frown, Marion's studying my clothes,

'I haven't got off to the best of starts, have I?" I sigh.

'Never-mind,' Marion assures, 'If you'd like to leave your CV, I'm sure Lucy will get back to you.' She's hesitating, 'Are your qualifications up to date?'

'More than you'd realise,' I smile back. My CV would need some careful editing before Lucy got to see it. "So, Lucy's had a baby girl. You don't know how much-it weighed do you?'

'No. I don't know how much she weighed.'

It's just for my Mum,' I lie, 'she loves details like that - and Lucy's an old friend of mine.'

'-Really?' Marion has stops sweeping and settles in a chair. 'So, how do you know Lucy?'

I'd known Lucy a long time ago, we'd gone to school together - or so I was told: I'd have been too young to remember that clearly.

Marion sounds intrigued, 'you went to school with Lucy?'

'She says I did,' I recall, 'I'd of spent most of the time with her at college, when I wasn't in the crèche.' I summarise, 'She said, if I was in the area, I should pop in and say Hi!'

'Not the best of timing!" Marion cheers, 'Would you like a cup of tea?

'I should get going..' I pull back, watching as rain spits down the window it's been threatening all morning: hence my wet weather leather ware.

'At least wait until it stops raining.' Marion's advising.

＊

'So,' Marion sat back reading my portfolio, 'you got your NVQ at college. Have you always been interested in hairdressing?'

Lucy had said that the hairdressing qualification was for both of us, our security. She'd inspired me when no-one else could; that image of her ankle deep in off cuts - and then she'd left my life as quickly as I'd popped into hers.

Marion's noticed something amiss in the files 'I see that you had to,' she fumbles with my folder, 'your course was interrupted?'

78

'That's right, I had to, drop out after around ten months.'

'-A family crisis?'

'-My Mum died. Heart-failure.'

'I'm sorry.' Marion studies me sadly, 'but you went back?'

I nod, 'I knew I'd have to go back one day and put things right, for Mum,' I hesitated, 'and Lucy could be very persuasive..'

'Can't she though?' Marion agrees, standing up she's about to rattle a gravy tin in my direction, then she remembers and drops a twenty pence from out her apron. 'I'll put yours in..' I hear the tin jangle as I count her chins.

'Lucy persuaded me,' Marion recalls, 'She thought of me straight away for this job.'

I must look amazed.

'It's true!' Marion beams, 'She said, "I don't want one of those dreary drop-outs. Why don't you come and work for me?".'

I brush tenderly at my nose-stud. 'Suddenly, I'm a cloche!' I smile grudgingly as Marion hands me Lucy's Tottenham Hotspur mug with two sugars.

'Oh, not you dear!' Marion laughs, 'Some customers might be, uncomfortable with it, can you take it out?'

I nod.

Marion smiles gently back at me, 'I'll let you into a secret,' her eyes light up.

'What?' She tilts to show me her crown.

'This hair, it isn't all mine and it used to be purple, confidence thing. Right?'

I nod again.

' Do you live close-by?'

'I'll be moving to the area..' I lie, 'What I mean is, I had family around here. I've always loved it.'

'Good!' Marion mentally ticks another box, 'Look at me conducting my first interview.'

'You're doing very well,'

'Thank you.' She pauses, 'Is there anything else you'd like to ask me?'

'Yes.' I hesitate. Slipping a hand in my pocket, I place a battery beside the cup. 'Where's your loo?'

79

Marion leads me upstairs to it.

The flat hadn't changed at all - not since my last visit. I couldn't help peering at the photos along the wall by the stairs: it was Lucy and her boyfriend taken about a year ago - that photo made me feel so close, perhaps closer than I'd ever been to my mother.

'Ah, that's Lucy,' Marion confirms, 'just after their engagement..' She sees me staring at Lucy's partner in the frame. '-And that's-.'

'-Robert.' I smile, 'Hello Dad!' I whisper.

'That's right!' Marion is amazed.

A strange rattling can be heard as we descend the stairs. Marion's frowning, she's glaring at me. I remain perplexed. She eagerly follows me down each stair and we shuffle out to the tearoom,

'What's going on?' She faces me coldly, 'If your friend is planning to,'

'-My friend?' I shake my head.

Marion is distracted by the front doorbell. She goes hesitantly, then her tone lightens. 'Just a tick,' she calls back. 'Goodness, you must be soaked, let me help.'

Hearing voices, I walk into the shop, freezing at the sight of the new mum in a green raincoat. 'Oh Marion, I didn't mean to frighten you..' She smiles nervously in my direction. 'There's a young man outside, is he anything to do with you?'

'A little,' I sigh, 'He's not causing trouble is he?'

'He was clearing boxes away from the door," Lucy recalls, looking at me confusedly. 'I'm sorry, we haven't..'

'Francesca,' I introduce myself, stepping forward to ease the carry-cot and place it onto the chair.

'Oh thank you,' she looks straight at me, 'Francesca's a lovely name,' she comments, 'you'll have to forgive me: but I don't recall..' She's struggling to remember my face, 'Francesca, I'm so sorry.'

'That's fine.' I assure her; She's just like I remember her, only tired and wet. 'Seven pounds four ounces can take a lot out of you..'

'It can indeed.' Lucy nods, 'I'm puffed!'

'Didn't Robert collect you?' Marion's looking confused. 'Don't tell me you came on the bus?'

'Don't fuss,' Lucy raises a tired hand. 'We both had time for a little nap,' she peers into the cot. 'Didn't we sweetheart?'

Marion briefs Lucy about our meeting and mentions my interest in the flat. By now, I'm peering into the carry-cot, yet there could be no mistaking that little chubby face, and those wisps of blond hair; She looked enchanting.

'Francesca,' Lucy addresses me directly for the first time. 'About the flat upstairs, it's not that you wouldn't be the perfect....' Lucy's struggling.

'-It's just that you feel rushed into making a decision?' I suggest timidly.

'That's Right,' Lucy breathes in, relieved I'm taking this so well. 'Can I contact you, later today?'

'That's fine..' I am disappointed, it was just by being here and moving into that flat upstairs that I'd hoped to change their destiny - now I'd have to opt for plan B .

'I'll just leave my details then,' so I did, and tucked in the congratulations card I've left a good will message I mention the item I left in the tearoom – batteries may seem a curious gift to leave for a little girl - no they aren't batteries for the baby monitor: or for the new dad's walkman - they are for the smoke detector – and not that I want to alarm her, she never listens anyway, but I've urged her to do something for the two of us and tell Dr Adams about those little sleepy spells.

You see I'd known long before I'd showed up there that Lucy had become a mum to a baby girl; and cuddled up in her favourite yellow blankie which Auntie Marion had knitted for her, I knew they'd both be fine now.

Early yesterday morning, Lucy had given birth to a baby girl, seven pounds four ounces - shortly to be christened Francesca Louise Barker – you see, that little girl - was me.

© 2005

WRITING WITH MY FREE HAND:

In 2003 I began a number of interesting vocations, I began working at a well known DIY STORE on the Isle of Wight and I was also finishing a project for Solent Tv on the difficulties of jobseeking on the Island.

This was shortly before a before a major improvement to the Island's buses and the rebuild of the bus station. I'm also including some tales with jobsearch as their theme.

Last Bus Leaving at Midnight
(Jo's version)

You know, it's an astonishing fact; but 50 Billion times every quarter of a second someone, somewhere makes a mistake: fortunately it isn't always destined to fry hapless astronauts - or make a bungie jumper kiss the concrete - but sometimes that mistake: will be made by you.

I'd had a mostly enjoyable first shift as a Customer Advisor - they'd finally given me some customers to advise, I could be gently pirouetted, chipping off customers one by one; in the circles they'd be standing scratching their heads.

"Let me know if you need any help...' I'd smile: and they did didn't they?

.So, you're sat back reading yester-weeks papers - when your concrete-layered new boss pops in just to decree that Mondays are your rostered day off.

So, then Judy offers me a lift to the bus stop - so I wouldn't miss it; you see, the last bus, that next one: is leaving at Midnight - So I'm not going to miss this one - and then your Boss says we can all go earlier - can your day get any better? Obviously not!

***

I was grateful to Judy, had I missed the 9.30 pm *from Stand F,* I'd of had serious concerns; a choice between the bogs, the boozer..*ah sorry, 'Social' Club* or the darkened night sky.

Why does it always pour down when you're waiting for a bus? The Timetable assures the bus is arriving any moment now at 20:40, I'd have just twenty-five minutes to savour the delights of how to tease Jemma with the delights of my unexpected rostered day off: she'd probably take it quite well, the fact is I'd only half expected it: there had been hints, obviously, talk of some big in store think tank where they plotted these things with Gulf War precision.

The night is cold, wet and dark and there are kids on the broken green plastic seats close by, sucking the tongue studs from each other, cringing as the seat digs into their passions. A frizzy-haired jean-clad bundle of lust gazes into her lovers inflamed eyes, she's rubbing her hip, she winces, 'That-bloody-hurt!' She gapes around, showing him the jagged seat spike, 'Flipping thing!' she throbs, searching for a better description as this night tinges red with profanity. They un-grope and notice me - so I shuffle over to the timetable.

Then I see him: I won't waste pointless explanatory detail, I mean you've all seen him: or her, standing beside you at the bus stop - they don't say anything: just try to look through you to read the darn thing - it's obvious what he wanted, so I quickly scan it - although there's no need, I've read it billions of times - and sure enough there it is ; I'd missed the 8pm but at 8.30pm, or 21:30 in speaking clock gibberish...

"Are you waiting for the next bus to *the West Wight*?" I confront him, "well, you have about two minutes," He thanks me graciously, and in the artificial light his bald head seems to shine and his gold tooth glimmers. He wanders off: to chat with fellow travellers.

As the 'kids' in front of me opt for a full-on snog I avert my eyes, search out my now aptly titled rainproof coat and I ponder - how the heck did I get so lucky?

*

"It's running a little late isn't it?" I summarise as our man crosses back over to me in his clod-crunching hiking boots and yellow rain-splashed T shirt, *I shall not mention his khaki shorts - whoops.*

"*-Just a little...*"; It's 8:41 pm and the only 8:30ish bus pulled in and parked ten minutes ago - then I comprehend what's happened: you see I've just realised, 8:40 pm wasn't on the times at the bus station - it was on the times for the little blue local bus outside work - and my eye gazes back to the board: and I realise 21:35 is nine thirty five.

I mean it always has been and I knew it was ; I've slipped out of

84

real time, I left work earlier than expected and never adjusted mentally to the new time - you see it made no difference to me: all I could do was buy a bottle of sprite and hang out at the bus depot until my bank credit transfer kicked in five weeks from tonight : but *Mr Khaki shorts* - he might of had plans; he might have a life anyway he's killing time further down the line - who next will he want to kill?

My heart is pounding. When he comes over: I'm just going to tell him outright - I mean, I'd pinned my hopes on that Saturday Night Explorer too; you try it: when you're next trapped at a Bus Stop on a piddling rain-lashed religious day of rest - and you know you can't afford to miss that bus that will actually take you home - imagine the Saturday Night Bus is going to arrive any moment...

But what a mistake to make - I reach into my black carry all and fumble for my well-read timetable, and there it is ; the 8.30pm does exactly what it says in this thing: sweeps into the Bus Station and then sits there grinning at us for the next hour: like a cheeky toddler knowing he's gonna get you in trouble - and he's spotted me.
    " *Did you misread that timetable?*" He blurts out, his eyes *warming with rage, so I apologise, he blanks me - and huffs off to drown his cliche's across the crossing at the anti-social's club.* "Thank-you very *much!*" He huffs, not stopping for me to explain about time anomalies, bended time; arriving earlier and not readjusting.

Eight people waiting for a two-hourly service bus on a sopping Sunday Night, *oh and one grump, just round the bend.* That says it all: about monopolies, oddity's and 'Keep Sunday (Blooming) Special' campaigns - bloody priceless isn't it? A local bus, a three minute journey five minutes from work - or a rather sweaty hobble of twenty minutes duration, is followed by a two hour soakathon or a sit down in the toilets - which reminds me...

85

My thirst heartily quenched after a five and a half hour virginal shift the bottle of Sprite takes it revenge, and can anyone tell me why you can never sit down in Men's toilets? I might have been tempted to stay here: wait for the next bus, at 23:30pm, but I decided to risk it, hopefully grumpy would be well-stupoured and would make some other arrangements.

*

If I had fastened my hopes on misery guts passing out, tough I saw him waddling out barely intoxicated just as the bus travelled the short three second journey to Stand F: so he does have friends, Thing is, he didn't let it go: *"I suggest you let us read the bus timetables ourselves in the future," He hisses* at me shortly before his twilight descent through the hydraulic doors – like an ill-judged gatecrasher on Stars in Their Eyes - difference is, then he's gone: only he isn't gone, "Tonight Matthew, I'm going to be a miserable excuse for a human being." - I mean honestly! He had plenty of time to read the timetable: I wasn't standing there with my hands covering it like a big jelly, nor was he standing next to me when I left the vehicle: but I feel he will always be there; taunting me to mess up an order, glowering over me when I'm about to tell someone the correct time - or when that next bus is : his words, they still hurt.

Later that week, Jemma wakes me from a daze, "You were having a nightmare," she eases, "Calling out," she asks, "what's happened?" So I tell her how I wish I could have handled that situation differently.

"Who'd have thought going home early could have such major repercussions?" She sighs brushing at my damp brow.

"I got it wrong, he chose to score another point: alright so, he didn't tell everyone on the bus I was numerically dyslexic: but..."

"-He may as well have done! " Jemma considers, "So having boiled over with it in your sleep, fumed about it, and finally discussed it with your soul-mate - what next?"

"Sorry?"

"You apologised twice to a pig of a man, and might as well have saved your breath,"

"-Too-right!"

"Yet, if he collapsed at your store, you'd try and help him, in a first aid emergency, or if he was trying to find a missing cat-"

"More so to make up for it-"

"So, what does that say about you?"

"Eh?"

"Only that you haven't changed, he: hasn't changed you, because you handled it wrongly; just an angry raging little man: but he hasn't won, don't you see?"

I clearly don't, so Jemma clutches my hand, "-He is clearly someone that has never made a mistake, and a less-rounded person?" She kisses between my fingers, "-I wouldn't want to know," Jemma reasons that if I had that moment again I would have learned from it, relive it, embrace the trillions of ways to improve it: and I will learn from it - and recover; I'll get over it.

She's right ; I shall cherish my little foibles, my minor glitches and little stumbles - I won't let him bully me; although I'll relive that moment a billion times.

And, when someone asks me the time of the next bus? I shall still tell them.

So, we reach scenario thirty-seven; it is my favourite and the one I created to supercede the previously filled encounter - it is my favourite: because it allows me to move on.

"I suggest you let us read our own timetables in the future!" he hisses - but this time I'm ready for him, before he descends.

"Excuse me!" I shout, and even the young lovers gape at me surprised,

"-But I'd like to call a poll vote-of-the-eight people here, tonight," I smile, "How many of you, looking at the bus station timetable absent-mindedly let their finger wander into Saturday

87

Night?" At first, reluctance, then: redemption.

"Anyone else?" I chime, "Come on, don't be shy, we've all done it. The other passengers finally admit to it : "A full house. Which makes us all fallible human beings -" and I scowl back at grumpy globe trotter, "And still makes you a complete idiot, Thank you and good night!"

He turns a crimson-tide and departs swiftly stage coach left - and we go softly on -until our next judder... © 2003

Job Hunter

Jill Dudley was a babe! - Not that I'm being sexist or nothink; that was my first impression. I'd had a week close to barracks; a severe weather warning on the telly, and I, like my career wasn't going nowhere.

It had all started with that flaming computer battery!

"Computers need batteries to run the clock," So the snotty little upstart of a repair man informing me it was the latest model. "I'll see you again in fifteen months," He says, smiling.

So my exile was over - no more sneaking to the Training Rooms to cadge a duplicate of my old CV ; Just as well as some of those details were every bit as sketchy as the contents on a diet product.

Anyway, for that week, it was attack of the mutant arm-ache, RSI they'd 'of called it in business circles; there was no time for graceful calligraphy, it was blotch and shove it into the envelope - my envelope payed for from my dole money - so anyway's: I was delighted when this cheery young woman rang me up.

'Mr Hunter, this is Jill Dudley from Sam's, concerning your application for Customer Advisor...'

'-Thank you very much for letting me know," I piped.

'We'd like to invite you to an interview, Tomorrow, at Twelve O' Clock..'

'Ah, but they're broadcasting heavy rain Tomorrow,'

'I know, but that is all right?'

'It's fine,' I try my best to assure her.

'Very good, you'll have to let Sally at the desk know you're here, and then she'll bring you to our office - are there any questions you'd like to ask me?'

'-Oh, no thank-you very much, I'll look forward to seeing you tomorrow, thank you, Sally...'; I know: it wasn't me, that cheery feel-good voice - and I know Sally was the girl at the counter: but it wasn't my fault - why didn't she say twelve noon? I'd be up half the night wondering if she'd meant me to come in the evening - you know, like those high street stores with their special video openings, they say you haven't lived until you've watched Harry Potter at five past midnight, well ho-hum...

***

So, well I wasn't quite sure what to wear - should I dress for the weather or for working in a, cleaners: and just what does Jill mean by Customer Advisor any-ways? From dredging up those scrawled notes it reads very much like a Sales Assistant to me; should I wear a tie - one of those clip-ons, in case someone grabs me by the throat?

I'm on time: but I needed to dodge those showers, so I leg it from the bus stop - and there's a poor little brat, barely three years old, bawling outside the local toy store - here it is, Sam's - right next to that well known brand of chemists where I couldn't find any Wellingtons.

There's a bit of a wait at the counter, Sally's talking to a customer - a white-haired old dear who sounds most particular about the temperature for a boil wash, anyway she shuffles off so I wodge myself forward.

'Hello, I'm here to see JIll about the advisor's job...'

They're soon having a brief discussion at the desk about who the hell Jill is - where upon 'Wendy' informs her troubled and bubbly colleague that Jill is the Regional Head.

'Oh yeah,' Sally's giggling, and she's chewing gum too - bad habit that; Well, I've just noticed on the Video Monitor above our heads, I've grown far more stubble than I'd realised when I'd been excising my chin two hours previously. After a brief interlude where Sally finds her notes I'm escorted into the Waiting Room.

"WAITING ROOM"; I'll make no secret of it, as they did, this was the storage cupboard wasn't it? As the Ironing board, coat racks and Supersud washing powder boxes made abundantly clear.

There are three of us awaiting our chance to shine - a grubby, snotty little berk with not quite a skinhead compelled by glasses any well meaning friend would step on; A blond haired crumpet who seems to think we've got nothing better to do than ogle her chest for the duration; Well actually, I've always been an ankles and thigh man

90

myself - and me, well you have to include yourself in any line up, don't you? And see what you can offer that the rest can't, well I'm standing on behalf of the Apathetic Party...

The busty lass is called Heidi, judging by the sticker on her left chest, and she's been scoffing lemon peppermints - and then there's 'super swot'; He holds his life between his hands in a black plastic-tied folder - he's crunching something too: must be his teeth and, in a bleak moment I realise that I haven't been given a sticker, that at least gives me some ambiguity; I'm the fuzz-ball with no name: and seemingly no shaving kit; although I finely groomed myself mere hours ago,,,

I'm about to launch into my regular spiel about how one never has time to read all the magazines, when - bloody hell, they've called me; I never even got a chance to find out the name of that dude in glasses!

*

'Good Morning Mr Hunter,' Jill, as I've said was a babe! A petite babe - she's dressed in a blue suit and dress, the standard dress for SAMS - she's sitting on a purple cushioned antique chair "I'm glad you made it, the weather wasn't too severe was it?'

The calm before the storm...

'No, I think I timed it just right,' I smile, just before I realise that with this face only my mother would hire me.

'That's fine,' She looks, a little severe - and coughs, 'Excuse me,' she brushes her throat as she edges back from her seat and fills two plastic beakers from a jug on the table.

'Please help yourself...' She offers me the jug after she's poured one - so I do, not even spilling it or anything and hoping my hands wouldn't shake - which might have been her plan, to put me off guard.

'So, tell me about yourself...' She smiles, and that's done it, if I hadn't been briefed by a professional I'd of mentioned everything barring my elastoplast allergy - and the bunnies we used to keep on the front lawn before, that incident with the dog.

'Well at the moment I'm a job hunter..' ;She laughs at my little

91

joke - and I'm not sure I even made one. 'I apply for everything I can..'

'-And, what appealed to you about this position?'

I go blank; Well that's quite rare for me - and I'm blushing as well, never a good look, 'Well the position appealed, to me..'

'Go, on..'

'Well,' suddenly inspiration, and I'm not letting go, 'it seems a, friendly place to work, the staff are, very bubbly - and it was fortuitously timed..'

'-You've been looking for something in customer Relations?' She bites eagerly.

'Oh yes!' And then I hesitate, 'Well what appealed? My comp-Word Processor failed - and this was a job where you had to send an application form, as well, as a CV..'

'Well that explains a point I wanted to raise,' she laughs, 'About why your CV finishes abruptly in 1996, where as your application form goes into great detail about your most recent position,' she coughs again, seizing me with her "Come to bed" oh no, we musn't! eyes.'-Well yes that does explain it,'; That and the fact there was a second sheet with additional details, and that seemingly bloody awful referee I'm not going to mention - on that page that either freezes or comes out   as gobbledegook when you try and print it.

'Well that shows some initiative!' She delights, 'especially here: you have to think on your feet,' another swig, 'I've noticed, you like to keep quite detailed notes..'

'-Never hurts..' I look up from my scrawling's.

So, we talk about my past vocations; I'm trying to put a Customer Advisor slant on everything: but at the end of the day it's still just a potato! And, she explains a little about the business, how many branches they have countrywide - and how, as I surmised, they're a very happy team.

'So,' she massages her throat and then sips her water.'Do you have any questions that you'd like to ask me?'

Not really; You see, I'd checked with a main rival around the corner: and checked in a book at the library that listed the skills I'd need, but this whiff of scorching plastic which I never located the source of, well it awakens my mind. You must always have a question apparently because it shows in most cases that you're still awake.

'Well it does say that you'll train me in all the areas...'; I gulp, '- But is there a special uniform I'd...'

'Oh, yes,' she nods; Call me Mr Fatalistic but I can't see myself in a blouse and skirt, she continues to assure me, 'There is a male variation of the uniform. We have some very successful male colleagues at some of our, other stores,'; She then adds something about group dynamics, which I didn't catch and you, frankly won't be interested in - and, to be honest, neither was I: not once Jill had made the word 'group' sound like grope.

Anyway, as I left my chair having prised my warm bottom from the upholstery, I realise Little Miss Peppermint Cruncher is in the frame - and both me and swot boy acknowledged this; Thing is I know what I did wrong - I should have popped into the Chemists and bought Jill some throat sweets: but I dithered about inappropriateness of actions, and how it might be seen as slightly sleazy to swot up to your interviewer. So, if you see me on the streets selling leaflets, or queuing in the November chill - you'll know that I'll always wonder if it was that moments hesitation outside the Chemists before the rain came..

The Spin -Cycle

'This always happens!' I growl, as my husband Roger puts his foot down, trying again to kick that engine into life.

We'd been waiting to go to that new DIY store that had just opened - and today was perfect for it!

'Well,' Roger considers, as he glances back, 'we haven't used the car in over a fortnight!' Then he smiles, 'Never mind Lind, at least we'll save a fortune on the old rubbish at the sales.'

"Old Rubbish!?" He hadn't beaten me yet! I unstrapped myself from the seatbelt, navigated myself around a pool of water on the car-mat and waded sure-footedly down the drive.

'Linda, where are you going?' Roger yells back; where does he think I'm going? After two weeks cooped up watching Christmas soaps - I'm making a claim on that big wide world again - the oxygen of commerce.

'I'll catch a bus!' I turn and shout back at him - I watch as Roger groans and waves me on.

That's right! A bus still runs every two hours even on public holidays - the bus company clearly understands how important my bargains are to me.

Last time, I'd found a lovely purple jumper; a bit frayed: but with twenty five pounds off I wasn't going to grumble, not like my daughter, Natalie - oh she'd been nice enough at Christmas unwrapping the thing - but it was a different matter when I caught her trying to bleach it!

'Oh mum!' She'd confessed, 'It was lovely, but I don't think it's my colour.'; Not that my beloved offspring had a "colour" - not unless it was green.

I'm still letting this all simmer gently through me as I wallow towards the bus stop and clamber to the shelter, I slither and squelch as you might imagine - but that's just like Natalie, making me fall in the mud when I'm thinking about her little quirks - that girl is so inconsiderate - and worse, Natalie hadn't only grown into a young adult: whatever that means, she'd developed a weakness for collection jars - especially for that last appeal on the telly. It's not that I'm not occasionally thoughtful and generous - I've always had a soft spot for Terry Wogan, no Natalie worries me, that girl's got to learn that it's not her job to save the planet.

Looking back along the road, I can't see any sign of a bus, so I fumble through my purse clutching longingly at my credit card and lovingly at the crisp fiver I keep for such emergencies.

***

'Where to, love?' The driver asks, now he's finally deigned to put in an appearance - he was probably washing the bus, it looks sparkling.

'Braden's Field?' I query.

'-The Shopping Centre?' He rolls his eyes, 'I'm only going to the station,' he explains in a patient manner you might usually reserve for overseas visitors and the chronically deaf, 'you'll have quite a walk to the shopping centre..'

'Yes, thank-you!' I acknowledge him and he persuades me to get a special return ticket and I shuffle on.

I'm not bothered about walking, it's brisk but sunny day and there are plenty of nice shops on the outskirts of town - and I'd get more done without my hubby's interference and sharp eye on the purse strings - and why should I be feeling guilty that Roger had put in all those extra hours to clear the credit card bills? It was only right that I should spend something on myself - that's why we have a credit card...

*

So, I'm struggling off the bus and straight into a dilemma; I've only got two hours and all the shops along the route seem so tempting, in no time at all I've found a lovely jumper and matching gloves, and a really stylish hat - but here's my quandary - do I have time to reach the Shopping Centre first, make my way to it - or see where the mood takes me?

While I'm making up my mind I browse the local bookshop, and

95

that's lucky - my favourite Author has a new book out, it's a hard-back, a little pricey but in the sale now on I can get a whole 10% off! 10 per cent - that's a bargain isn't it?

One minor hindrance, on the way out a young man with a severe crew-cut blocks my way.

'Cancer Relief?' He shakes his tin.

'Sorry,' I barge away, 'um I don't have any change,' I lie - shortly afterwards I see him stagger over to the bench in the square,

'Excuse me,' a kindly voice jangles. 'Would you like to buy a copy of The Big Iss-'

'I haven't time, shopping!' I growl – letting another burly figure bundled in jumpers jump to the side. 'Honestly!' I shake my head sadly, when you're shopping time's always at a premium.

As I reach the Shopping Centre I stare in at my favourite store, Finlay's Ladies-wear: they have the most beautiful pair of black shoes with gold edging : and I'm salivating at the window, licking my lips as it were, shoes you see have always been my Achilles Heel - now they are nice: and I'm fairly sure that if Natalie asks nicely I'll let her borrow them.

Not that Natalie will ever understand, but buying nice clothes and shoes in particular - well they make me feel confident, sexy and special: Natalie certainly doesn't lack in confidence - but while that strange young man with staring eyes; had reached me - Natalie was more subtle, Tinking back, I'm recalling her pale weathered face; frozen fingers poking through fingerless green gloves; like sausages just out the freezer - her look pleadingly but understanding.

My daughter it seems to me has become my moral dimension - why couldn't she have a good time without feeling guilty about it? To have a younger image of yourself with your husband's nose to keep you in check - well, it is so disconcerting!

To be fair, Natalie seldom rattles a tin, just places it on the table - so I can keep looking at it, coaxing me; leading me; working on my subconscious, *"Well, I can't force you: but, all the money that you give blah blah blah,,"* Well she hasn't broken down my barriers in a long time - and she won't start now..

I hadn't realised how fast the time had passed, I glare at my watch with disbelief because I don't want to miss that bus - luckily, there it is waiting for me.

'Hello,' I smile, stepping on board with all my lovely purchases,

I shake my head; Natalie just glared at me last week I'd thrown out a carrier bag, then she'd said something about how I was helping to destroy the Ozone layer; that's just ridiculous - how can keeping one carrier bag save the universe? Anyway, if you ask me, we'd be better off without this ozone layer - time was when I could just lay out on a beach towel and not feel guilty about it; since we've had this ozone layer you can't even put out the washing without a dollop of sun cream on your back. Taking my seat I ease back, 'Oh, this has been quite an adventure!' I smile to myself, I'm not too sure of the trip home but I'm hopeful it will be scenic - and, it was certainly going to be! Ten minutes into the journey the driver pulls in at a bus stop.

'Sorry love, you'll have to get off here!' The driver advises with a jaded smile.

'I'm sorry?' I can't have heard him right.

'This bus doesn't go any further..' The driver patiently explains how the route had changed to reflect the Bank Holiday nature of the time-table.

' -But, I bought a special ticket,' I'm soon rummaging through my purse - and then my thick coat pockets, sure enough here it is - so I decide to show it again to the idiot: it seems he's even less interested.

'This bus doesn't go any further,' he repeats as the first dribbles of rain spit on the window, 'it waits twenty nine minutes then goes back to town.'

'-And what do I do?' I want to scream at him.

'There's another bus across the road.' The driver cheers up as the sun briefly puts in an appearance.

'Thank you..' I smile, and prepare to shuffle onto the platform -

I can see the other shelter just across the road and with luck I'll miss the downpours.

***

97

'How long until it arrives?' I splodge back through the rain soaked shelter to the driver who hasn't moved and is clearly tackling a fishy lunch, mackerel in your sandwiches - isn't that the height of extravagance? The driver sees me, and begins to scrutinise his timetable - before looking up shamefaced.

'It will be here in fifty eight minutes.' He closes the door.

'Thank you!' I hiss, in no time at all I've hobbled back to my shelter from across the road, and I sit there, dripping. I'm still dripping ten minutes later when I open my bag to pass the time ogling my purchases - then I pause. The book is nice enough - true I'd saved two pounds: but Natalie usually got me the paperback version for Mother's Day - a tradition you might say; now I'd have to fake appreciation – sad. The jumper wouldn't fit Robert: and anyway, he hates 'V' necks - and the gloves, even in this light you can see they were faded, that was probably why they were reduced.

I'd hoped that seizing the initiative and going shopping would be an adventure, I sighed, 'Dry off, get wet, dry off, trolley in the back of the ankles,' I shake my head at the painful memory, 'I'm stuck in the spin cycle!' I reasoned. Why did it always happen to me - I'd of had a better day enjoying Robert's company, or even just studying the washing machine.

Wading back over to the bus I glance in at the driver

'So, you're going back to town?' I ask hopefully.

'That's right,' he nods, 'Did you misread the time table?' He asked me sweetly.

'Oh I think I've been misreading them all my life..' I explain sadly...

***

Anyway, it didn't take that long to get back to the town. I thanked the driver and set off for the main precinct: and there they were, the most beautiful pair of black shoes with gold motif, I could do with another pair: as I'm looking down at my feet they positively ache just thinking of them, last years pair are looking tatty.

'A nice new pair of shoes might..' I'm hesitating because reflected in the glass is an image from the nearby charity shop - starving children are staring back at me - I turn away, hovering, and my mind is made up. I'm going in.

'Pardon Miss,' someone's grabbing at me.

'-What do you want?' I glare back – it's the wide-eyed boy from earlier – and he's holding my credit card.

'George says you dropped this earlier,' the boy recalls, 'in your rush to-'

'Oh, thank you,' I grimace as he hands it back to me, 'Why couldn't George have returned this?'

The boy gulps. 'Oh George thought I should take it to the police – didn't want to return it personally in case you were aggressive.'

'Oh nonsense,' I scoff, 'I'm unpleasant to everyone when I'm shopping, I don't mean anything by it..' I hesitate, 'I suppose George will be wanting a thank you.' I sigh, 'What do young men like these days?'

'You haven't met George have you?' He grins.

So, I shuffle forward, and considering George has been out in the elements, I consider he's looking quite well fed – and I meet George's eyes. 'Oh,' I blink, 'My mistake..'

*

You know, it's strange – Natalie's off saving the planet and I'm trundling along saving the pennies – I mean, what was going to do with ten copies of The Big Issue? Anyway, you can see my

point; it wasn't my fault George has run out of change – so I'm feeling guilty recalling those far-reaching patient eyes and those fingerless gloves – when I get this idea

*

'Hello Dear, this is 'George'.' I introduce them.

You see I've quite given up on Natalie making me a granny, so

99

this seems the perfect solution – our guest can have the spare room, it's only full of all my old shoes.

Robert grudgingly helps me to bundle the lot in some binliners and he's very quickly accepting of our new house guest – it will be good to have someone else to talk to – and you never know, Georgia might yet make me an honorary grandparent.

notes: I'll let you into a little secret about this story – People's Friend gave me some very wise advice about it not being interesting enough for their readers – so I re-worked it, adding George - and they were right..

In 2004 while I was finding my writing style, I came up with all sorts of experimental tales that simply weren't commercial but helped to add to that feeling of accomplishment on my days off – commercial success can always come later..Also, I was trying to master that most commercial of short stories - the tale with a twist..

Roller Coaster Ride

Now, I don't like roller coasters - it's a funny thing: well, no it isn't - I base it on two things; an episode of that dreams come true Prozac - where these cub scouts, for reasons best kept to themselves wanted to eat their lunch on a roller coaster; and then there's that nasty experience back in the Seventies at Fantasia World in Germany; I've never seen that shade of green since; the only thing that even came close was when Lou Ferrigno's colourist had an off day.

So, no, put simply Roller Coasters? Not for me

School trips? Weren't for me either! Tangled guts and other-worldly expressions were not in wonderment at the Dinosaur bones in the Natural History Museum, they were from the pretty sure state of paralysis inflicted when you never like to use strange toilets. So my wonder years were a blur; I didn't live them - and I take no joy at what that aggressive nasty little sod got up to - it was Becky who woke me from my daze.

"Hi Martin!" She would smile, in the lunch-room every day when all the others were ignoring me .

"-Hi Becks!" I'd grin - see, I could talk to girls, I just couldn't say anything profound and or the least bit enlightening; It might just have been her eyes, this flowing red head held me entranced, my lips quivering, hoping that my gob wouldn't explode.

And, I was safe enough for her to sit next to, without the slightest hint of anyone thinking there was a sexual chemistry between us: like I'd wish.

By half past twelve it was all seats taken. What choice did she have? It was me or Dave the predator - on the fertility seat, I had my problems, trying to think up interesting ways to get apple pips out of my teeth - and making my banana seem less erotic: but Dave? She'd of been eating Dave with her nimble flavoured sandwiches - and that was just too much for her to stomach.

So, Becky wooed me; not massively: but passively, she'd sit and work with me on art projects - and very occasionally, hold my hand to help me across the road.

"This is my best friend, Martin!" She'd introduce me, even to her Mum at the School Jumble Sales - and woe betide if Dave tried to come between us - she'd cripple anyone with her steel toe-capped shoes, or did it just seem like that?

When we did get a moment alone she'd subtly boost my confidence "You could be even more attractive if you wore Contact Lenses," She'd coo, "Do you like it when I hold your hand?" She asked, only once.

At Christmas, she'd try to shove me under the Mistletoe - only I'd become like a big dollop all bashful and shy - and the kiss was very quick, and disappointingly Brotherly.

"Oh Becky, don't be a bitch!" Julie, a Hazel-haired moppet from Class Twelve just glared at her. Things were obviously warming up between us.

Then...When we came back from Christmas Holidays, and our little fling was like the ground, black Ice, all over, bloody dangerous and I started to fear her spiked toes. Becky was kinder to Dave though, seemed quite insistent that I should let him tug along, probably to amuse her - everything he said made her laugh, including when he was kidding about me.

That term, she boosted his confidence by letting him work on a project together - a beautiful 2D figure in paper-mache and Plaster of Paris - they clearly had a good working chemistry, although she still liked to let me carry her bag.

One day however, when it was really hot - her and Julie exchange mischievous glances and Becky jumps on me, putting her arms around my neck - I thought it was wow, although at later reunions I learned she'd been suitably compensated.

I think it all went wrong for us at Alton Towers, we went there one day in the holidays, me Dave and bubbly Becky, that I started to call her after the incident when the champagne cork had got lodged in her nose - thing is, I trusted that Dave would look after her, I went green at the thought of all those steps - and she laughs and grudgingly allows Dave to escort her - and that was that.

102

In a way it's a good thing I didn't go on that Holiday to Wales with the rest of my form. Daredevil Dave broke his leg in oh so many places, and that ruined the trip: Becky feeling all so responsible for our friend spent the night with him until help came and ended up making herself ill, very ill, she had morning sickness actually...

Thing is as I look back now, I see that Ronan Keating had it right, 'life is a roller coaster' and while I'm blessed with both limbs, fantastically improved glasses, and have a close and loving family, I'm blessed, not blessed with Children or a Girlfriend or even a wife, but you can't have everything.

Poor Becky's really been through the wars; Three Children, a house and a husband that convinced her to move to Beverly Hills, before deciding he preferred to be called Davina - then there's me, dependable, 'marvellous' Martin - I'm devoted to my job, I've found I don't really need to drink - or socialise, and some people have even called me a loner: but I'll ask you this - which one of us is happier?

© 2004

Separation Anxiety

'Is there something wrong?' I gulped. The receptionist, a young thing who seemed never to have spoken to another adult her entire life, was smiling as if I had just made an hilarious joke. As you might imagine after the long trip round the car-park, wrestling with that gearstick to shift into second gear, the long wait at the door and finally those wretched buzzers - I was in no mood for humour.

'This, doesn't look very much like you..' She sighs, showing me the brazen hussy newly cropped from the old passport: our trip to Spain, when yes I had been young-er.

'It was taken a while ago...' I blustered.

'-It's black and white...'

'That's what I mean!' She grimaces. '-And you said you have an important package you wanted to deliver to Robert Hill: can I see the package?'

'-I left it in the car..' I explain apologetically; Robert had told me what to expect, I recalled, trying to calm myself, but I hadn't expected all this security - I had phoned ahead to clear everything. 'What do you need now - a urine sample?'

'There's no need to be sarcastic Miss..' she blinks.

'- It's Mrs, you called me "Miss", I really hate that when someone just assumes...'

' I'm sorry.' She pats the visitors book, leaning over it to examine my scrawl. ' Again, I'm sorry if you feel I've been abrupt with you.' She explains that her previous experience had been with Nursery Groups and that I had raised her concerns, hence the alarm bells and the need to double-check.. 'Robert's position here can make him a target for undesirables, I wouldn't be doing my job if I didn't-' she frowns, 'you must have spoken to our Senior Receptionist, Brenda.'

'That's right..' I recall the chirpy old dear telling me it was completely alright and that she'd even put the kettle on for me whenever I arrived. 'I'm sure she'd say it was alright...'

She had to leave early. She had one of her migraines, I can't say I'm that surprised!'

'Yes, that's right,' I smile, 'an elderly woman with white hair, I remember her. She didn't look very happy either: just stared back at me, didn't say a word.'

'Brenda?!'

I've surprised her: but I've been thinking on my feet. 'I know what this is all about, last time I took Robert off site, there were problems..'

'-It can be disruptive, your son has to settle into the routine, adjust to the-'

'-Monotony?'

'You're not making things easy, Mrs Hill the rules are he cannot leave the grounds without prior arrangement: and that we have to check any items being bought in.'

'It was his lunch okay!' Now I've told her, 'I bought him lunch!' I despair, 'I thought we'd sit outside and have lunch.'He says all that refined stuff is poisoning him, you know how young men can be about their food?'

She says she does, then she wants to make a note of any allergies for her records.

'This is ridiculous, I know his room number. I can wait for him in the library...'

'-Mrs Hill, I'm afraid that until you can verify who you are I cannot allow you into any of the rooms.'

'Really? I ' start to take in my surroundings, I know exactly where he is just need to get my bearings, I start to making a dash for it - but she's too quick, her shrill voice freezes me.

'Mrs Hill if you go into any of those rooms unauthorised, you'll be escorted from the premises.'

I stand shocked; She is joking isn't she? She wouldn't then I see in her eyes - she would, little jobs-worth! I could hardly dare think of my little Robbie trapped here with these thugs - I'd come to set him free.

'You'll have to come back later!'

'Later!' I was seeing red, 'Do you know how difficult parking is around here? You have to get here fifteen minutes early just to avoid being twenty minutes late!' She's wavering, I can see she's wavering, any minute now Miss high and mighty's going to come out of her box and then I've got her right where I want her: I feel sorry for her in a way...

'I'm not unsympathetic..' she brushes her wrist, 'and there's no suggestion you'd knowingly harm Robert,' she slips out into the corridor, I'm spoiling for a fight: and then her phone rings.

'Barbara?' She frowns and nods knowingly, then she puts down the phone and walks over to me. 'Mrs Hill, I'm sorry...' She smiles, oddly,

'That was Barbara the woman you spoke to earlier, she says you do have a photo in your wallet...Sure enough, there it is, in my pocket: me and him smiling to the camera.

'Oh, I, er understand ' the receptionist says gently, 'I'm sorry for the mix up: I'll take you to see him now...'

'So I should think!' I huffed.

She goes in this room first, then when she comes out I know that something's wrong. She says Robert's just popped to the loo.

'Mum!' He comes dashing towards me, then wrapping his arms around me - it's so nice to get any reaction, he looks more grown up than last time I visited.

'I'm taking you home!' I say determinedly, '-They wouldn't let me see you: it's best for you to be at home with, us, the people that love you!'

Mrs fancy-talk receptionist is giving me the evil eye, Robert wants to go and talk to her.'How long do we have before you have to be back?'

'Mum, have you been borrowing Dad's car keys again?' He smiles.'Well you know there's always been a bit of rebel in me: shall we go for lunch?''I have to stay here Mum, you know it's for the best...' He shakes his head, 'We both agreed it was the best place for both of us..' He kisses me and I feel the sandpaper-effect of his ginger-stubble, then, he hugs me, '-but if you keep sneaking off in Dad's car whenever he comes to visit you, we'll have to think again...' He croaks. 'I don't know how-long, I can carry on teaching, if you're going to keep going walkabout!?'

© 2003

Our Day in the Sun (Full Version)

We don't want to sit in the sun because it's too hot, apparently; the UV rays will fry us in our seats. We can't stay in the car, because there's not enough ventilation - and it's black: like travelling about in a hearse, I don't know why you bought it - yes, I do.

One hour ago we were walking: a timely stroll around the deck of the car ferry.

You'd been moaning that you didn't see the point of getting out: that you felt safer in your car - left it so long that you had to perform a belly-dancing shuffle manoeuvre that made you clonk your knee on the inner seal: serves you right if you'd been stuck there. I don't remember our back seat drivers' ever being that childish.

So we're strolling along the deck, I'm taking deep cleansing breaths, finding the whole thing exhilarating, while you're still bellyaching about the chalets; they were perfectly acceptable. You have to expect ants at this time of year: and anyway our next door neighbours had far more to worry about, a one-year-old baby girl, who'd been teething! Well, ever since, you've been threatening to ring "Watchdog".

As we turn away from the deck, I tell you how refreshing it is breathing in fresh sea air that knows no bounds, so, you take out a cigarette, and smoke it right in front of me: you know how much it annoys me - after all your problems.

'I wish you wouldn't," I study you sadly. That's your cue to puff smoke in my face.

Soon, you're shaking your head in disapproval, at the "couple" in front on the deck.

'What does she see in him?' you ask me, pointing to, "that long-haired layabout." Where you see a child, barely a young woman herself, I see a young mother; her brown hair caught in the wind, holding their baby by the hand and looking out to sea, she almost heard you, and you know it: but as you turned your head away in disgust: I could see that she was lost in his smile...

One hour later, you're hungry, so god help us all, you'll need feeding! The road is long and empty, completely deserted for miles around. The restaurant and bar just appear out of nowhere, taking us both by surprise.

'It's like the end of the world...' I breathe in sharply and you tell me off for having such a sinister imagination.

'Let's stop for a bite to eat!' You suggest to me and so that's all agreed then.

***

The driveway's nearly unending and the car park's half empty: so you expect we're sure of a quick feed. I loved the island air, but I've missed the smell of petrol. The garden has many green wooden seats dotted around it, and you're excited.

'I'm going to sit in the garden!' you glare challengingly, '-And have a pint of beer!'

'You're, driving!' I remind you, and then you sulk, pulling out your cigarettes and lighting one.

'I'll have a sodden shandy then!' You grouch at me, before folding your arms.

Absent-mindedly I touch the car boot, it's hot and I pull my hand away. It's warmer than you've been all holiday - may as well have bought a hot water bottle, the comfort you've been.

'Look, who's arrived...' You hiss sardonically. And then you're watching her, the fragile dark-haired young woman, she's pushing a buggy. She glares at us with that determined grimace you only give when you've barged around a million supermarkets and only found one brand of nappy: the ones that seep at the edges.

And then, I've lost you, maybe you want to step forward and help the boyfriend to hold open the doors, smile at their baby: but you don't do you? Just grouch, I can't persuade you to wear the sun-hat and you won't even take off your jacket until we get in the cool, you, funny man.

We could have sat next to her, I'd have liked that, but you never can get too close can you? You never were any good with other people's children. The seats by the bar are the longest, made of solid wood with purple cushions; they look the most comfortable and there are paintings above them that will be lost on a baby: real art.

They're looking over at us, and I'm sure she wants to chat: she looks tired, I know they've been arguing; you can sense it through their body language.

'Oh, I'll have the chicken with pomfret's...'; the acne-troubled youth at the bar gives you a look like a cow being milked by cold hands: I keep trying to tell you this is not the place for your humour: there was never a place for it: and I'm sure there's no need to snap the plastic-coated menu.

'Will it be long?'

'Will it be long?' Does it matter?

The boyfriend's gone to the toilet now, leaving her to struggle with those silly glass containers. I would have liked to have talked to her but you'd of said I was being nosey. The baby has the sweetest smile, I know all babies do but she is something special.

I would have liked to have congratulated her on their lovely baby, could have explained about how I never had a daughter: that it wasn't meant to be, I could have explained about our family, the son you don't like to talk about: they say that talking helps; but you didn't like talking, men never do, that was the problem, don't let it out just sit and grouch about it; we may as well be strangers.

Now, the child is "screeching", and no, I don't know why. Maybe it's to do with you, staring at it, at her in that condescending way. You never used to be like that. You got so much pleasure from children.

'-Just a nice quiet meal...'; You scoff, 'Look at her, it's obvious why she's crying. She's got no rapport with the child...'; You become increasingly irritate. 'No wonder at it, the father's a dunderhead...'

I glare at you and that says enough.

It seems almost fated: that we shall sit in many places just like this, after going to our holiday retreat: and you'll get sulky as girls and boys just like those ones in front of us, grow bigger and bigger, the gap between us will grow larger and larger: but I'll go along to

109

keep the peace - because these breaks are so, important: and you'll still, keep moaning how "whingeing children" have ruined "your" holiday.

'Once was enough.' you said: then you changed your mind, what you meant was once was enough with me. I wanted to adopt: but it was too late for me; too late for us.

It's strange. A daughter would have made our family complete: and ironically she has done: I've had to accept her into our family: and yes she's grown up and taken up with some irresponsible 'little git': so what? It was "me" she came running to when she'd made that "terrible mistake."; I'm the one that knows where she's ticklish; why she took to wearing that neck scarf after the fifth form disco; and I had to explain that, no, she wasn't dying...

When I look at her, I don't see you begging me to take you back; explaining about the woman who didn't mean "anything"; how could the two of you have made a child so compassionate and loving? ; Strange, how you conjured up the required emotions at her mother's funeral.

You say, I'm "taking sides", just like you did over her belly button ring? ; Well, however will you be able to heal this rift that now exists between you, if you won't make the effort? Just how will things ever change between "us" if you won't sit down with this "endearing stranger" stop moaning and thank her for our lovely holiday - and "our" beautiful granddaughter?

Just Waiting

'Miss Hallett, take a seat please. Surgery's running a little late this morning...'.*Patronising crab! Some people just patronise you with their eyes don't they?*

Cor, I hate this, talking to myself: I'm my own worst company: The only woman here; those plants are wilting, I know how they feel. I hope they hurry up, 'cause I'm dying to go to the loo. Sat opposite, is an elderly gent who's clicking his teeth (I bet they're not 'his' teeth).

Oh no Josie Hallett, don't go falling into that trap. Not all old men are dirty old men, bet he's just as frightened as you are - he's not looking at my legs is he?

I should read a magazine: but I'd never manage to concentrate.; a magazine is like a friend: keeping you company while you wait. Can't just bring anyone, or read anything.

Probably not a good idea to read some of those stories anyway, I'm fragile at the moment; suites you being gloomy Josie, they always have some lovely stories, or cheery kids, wearing buckets on their heads; the health section's the worst: I know more about the male reproduction system than I want to thank you very much! Looks like I'm stuck with Reader's Digest, anyway, I've read all the others last time. *That's it. Go-away and stop leering at me!*

I can hear kids playing next door, must be the church playgroup - still, I'll have to get used to that. They sound noisy, but they're having fun. I saw a programme last night on parents' smacking their children, I'd never smack my child, they're too precious, so fragile - especially after last time. I wish Gav was here: he was really good when I told him."Don't worry love. We'll cope. We can afford it!"; I like that; Gavin is one-part, my lover and one-part my personal accountant. The thrill of being woken up at 2am will make it all worthwhile for him - yeah, right! Of course we'll "cope": but they'll have to be some prioritising.

Gavin wasn't much of a lover last night. He must have been

downstairs doing the books. It's always worse when you have things on your mind, and he must have guessed. I can't read music: but I can follow the tune, and when he finally came upstairs - it was like we weren't following the tune together, exhausting. Never knowing where those notes would take us or, how knackered, we would be when we got there; that reminds me, spray cream and toilet rolls, I must make a note. Those plants really don't look very healthy do they?

I wish Gavin was here, holding my hand and telling me, it's all going to be fine. I can smell the fake leather of his jacket just thinking about him; brushing my fingers through his short-cropped hair; kissing his fish and chip stained teeth. I hope the baby inherits his teeth rather than mine: but please god, let it have my ears; still, long as it's healthy that's the important thing...

Gangway, I need the loo...

***

Ah, that's better: I'll have to get used to doing that more often. I wonder if I'll ever be brave enough to breastfeed in public? The thing is, it's going to cause some changes, all the things Gavin loves about me they might, go west.

I hope he doesn't have cold hands, being prodded about is bad enough; if there's any danger then I won't go through with it; still, they'll advise me: don't know how many yet, when we know we can plan for it...

'Mrs Hallett, if you'd like to...you know where to go?'

'-Along the corridor?'

'First on the right...'

Gulp. It's my turn, arms to my side; best-foot forward; deep-cleansing, breath. Come on Josie! Don't let him see the fear: but, why am I scared? I'm the one having this baby and I'm going to protect it: and part of that is teaching 'it' not to fear those in

112

authority, I'm not going to let us get pushed around! Right, deep breath, knock on the door...

'Come in!'

***

I'm giddy as I stumble back into the waiting room, then I get my first big surprise.

'Gavin!' He's walking over to me gingerly, giving me a hug.

'Love?'; the look in my eyes is the only clue he needs. 'Thank-god!'; He's showing far more affection than I anticipated.

'-And, they're sure? I mean, there are no complications?'

I lead him into the corner and whisper sweetly into his ear.

'-How many?' Gavin asks tenderly.'-Four or Five!'

'Four!' I say with a smile.

'Ms Hallett?' The receptionist is smiling warmly. 'You're looking very pleased with yourself, is it, another, appointment in six months time?'

'Can I, get back to you on that, this afternoon?'

The receptionist looks at me blankly, then smiles warmly: I've never noticed how warm she was before.

'Of course!'

'We just have to go back and check our cover plan...' Gavin explains to the receptionist, 'I was in there with her, but all that medical stuff makes me, queasy?' The receptionist agrees with him.'But, I'm sure it's worth it!' Gavin reasons. 'She'll have a lovely smile. I'm so proud of her she hates people poking her around.' Then, he skulks off to read some medical leaflets.

'My boyfriend thought he'd have to re-mortgage the house to pay my dental bill...' I explain excitedly, 'I haven't told him yet, but he's got off lightly. Can you keep a secret?'

'Of course!' The receptionist nods indignantly.

'I've postponed the fillings because there's going to be a happy event...'; Gavin's frowning across at us, so I lean closer to the reception window.

'Oh I see,'

113

'I'm dying to tell Gavin, but I'm going to the doctor's, this afternoon, having it all confirmed.'

'Well, congratulations, I hope.'

'Thank you! I hope Gav gives up those early shifts because, when Baby comes, I'm going to need my rest.'

'Yes,' she says: and then she frowns and adds, "I'm sure you will!"; And I'm still trying to work out what she meant by that: maybe it was just the way she said it...

A Matter of Politics

'I'm really very embarrassed,' I breathe in, 'but when I saw the news, well, it all fitted..'

'The time and the place - and the video footage?' The Officer is comparing his notes. 'You say she's done a lot of this sort of thing?'

'Protest?' I scoff, 'Oh yes, it's something young girls do, isn't it?'

'You'd be surprised.'

'She'll hate me for it,' I'm soon letting out a sigh, 'but she's so determined,' I gulp, 'sometimes, she frightens me.' I'm so relieved to talk to someone about this - to be letting it all out at last.'She blanks me, she looks straight through me, you'd never guess that we were family.'

'So, you saw it on the news?' The officer sways his hand enticing me to go on.

'That's right, yes!' I reach forward for the glass of water the investigating Officer has placed on the table - I'm so grateful, the words are soon flowing, just like the water from that glass. 'I remembered her telling me!' I recall.

'How she wanted to get a good view. How she wanted to see the colour of his eyes..'; how she'd done it before, joined a crowd of supporters so their defences were down.'

The Officer is glancing into the carrier bag; it was still red, and I knew how embarrassed he felt to be looking through it, just studying the contents. 'Not your-average overnight bag is it?' He's trying to smile - but probably doesn't think the occasion warrants it.

'Will she go to prison?' I close my eyes and think about what I've done, 'It's assault isn't it?'

'Attempted assault,' the Officer seems to be considering the matter.' I'd like to think her age would go against that.' He's nodding that it could be a possibility..

'She'll hate me for this!' I croak, recalling a past that was never easy and has became increasingly more unchecked the older she has

115

got. 'It's just she's always been rebellious, I saw it and I just snapped!'

'It would be better for us, if she comes clean voluntarily.'

'-But, he'll want to press charges, won't he?'

'I don't know, Miss, er Madam.' He shakes his head as he reads his notes. 'An inch or two either way and it could have been his eye,' he calms down, 'I'm sure you're aware how serious this could have been?'

'Yes I am!' I groan, 'Just what do you think I should do? She's too big for me to smack her bottom, she won't listen to me, that's why I came to you!'

'Have you considered, talking to someone, a mediation session maybe?'

'-And, would you want to mediate with your mother?' I glare back at them and I can see on their faces - they think it's a bad idea too.

The door is opening as I speak and the desk Sergeant is coming in, there's a brief conversation then smiles all around - it seems there's good news.

'Gina's made a full confession,' the Officer informs me, 'but it seems the gentleman in question won't be pressing charges - it appears he wants to put the whole unpleasant incident behind him.' The Officer pauses, '-But he'd like Gina to meet with him and explain her grievances.'

'I'm sure she will,' I smile. 'Can you tell him that's very gracious of him?' They are soon frowning between themselves.

***

'You don't know how lucky you are?' I'm glaring at her.

'They blew it all out of proportion!' She's pulling her hand away, and then she mutters something about how the hooligan element always spoil things.

'I'm ashamed of you!' I'm growling at her, 'it's about time you learned to take responsibility for your actions!'

'Well, you can do that now,' she's hissing back at me, 'when they're fitting me with a tag and threatening to lock me up.'

They weren't going to press charges: but I insisted, when she refused to explain her actions; I was at the end of my rope.

"'It's the hooligan element",' I'm shaking my head and try not to look at her.'What did you expect?' I explode with my fury, she never listens to me - and my protests may as well be falling on deaf ears.

Mum's been bound over to "keep the peace" - and she can't believe her luck either, I'll say she's got off lightly, especially as she's been caught trying to hurl tomatoes at the Prime Minister!

This particular tale started life as one of those popular 60 word fiction tales that you sometimes still see in magazines – and so did the next tale, 'Uneasy Journey' which was extended from its first appearance as 'An Uneasy Passenger' in Chat in 2002. I'd like to thank Paul and all the staff at the Cabin in Freshwater and the lady who donated her copy of Chat so I could see my story in print.

An Uneasy Journey

"It's not natural mother!" My daughter Tina, is despairing; we were on our way back from the shops, walking back across the kids' playground, when she spots Kevin with his mates -right under her nose - or so Tina says: we live a good two minutes away: long enough to boil an egg so that's elevenses sorted out, "Do you think he might be having a problem with girls?"

"Girls' are always a problem," I point out. Tina was when she was a teenager: she would eat these fad foods just to get up her father's snout, chock ice and chips, I swear they made her spotty. "Kevin's a good boy!" I assure her: at least I know he won't come home and find him in bed with that terrible drummer who never took his boots off.

"He's bound to shy away and want to follow the gang, that's what all Seventeen Year-Olds want to do,"

"-But what if it's more than that?" Tina begins demolishing her egg, really letting the shell have it to make a slimy yellow mess that dribbles all over her plate. "What if he's, it's just: he always out with them down town, and then there's that birthday present he got me,"

I'm puzzled, my face must appear just as flummoxed. "Very, nice?"; I don't know what she expects me to say.

"-Wasn't it? Really. Where does he get the money for stuff like that?" She brushes at her ear, that nervous way she always does when she's talking about money. "It's not as if he's planning for the future.

"-Well if you must know, it was a loan.."

"You've *loaned* him, money?" Tina sighs, "How do you know he's not using it for other thing "Oh, you mean drugs?"

I shake my head, "How do I know? Because I trust him, we have an understanding..."

Tina looks up with a naive smile, "You-make-sure, he pays you back..."

"Yes dear, because that always happens: our Kevin's a good boy,"

"I suppose you're right: I didn't find anything in his room,"

118

She pauses, "That's really worrying, I used to hide things in this place you never found out about-"

"-The box on top of the wardrobe, as I recall..."; She always had better informed magazines than I did: she still has them now: but they are down beside the fire for everyone to read, rather than being squashed in that shoe box with Mills and Boon's stuffed on top.

Tina's gone all red, "How did you?"

"A mother knows dear," I explain patiently. "So what makes you think Kevin might be taking drugs?"

"Mood-swings," She summarises, "and he's always so, he never uses the phone in the house, always on his mobile - and Peter saw that message on the screen."

"A text message?"

"Something about meeting T outside W 5pm with cash, I mean what does that mean?"

I point out that though my darling husband managed to learn German and French I've barely mastered the Internet - never mind the secret language known as text.

"Well, there's one way to put your mind at rest-"

"-A private detective?"

She's joking isn't she? Please tell me she's joking: but no, she's been searching the classifieds for a specialist in surveillance procedures."That's a bit drastic dear. Why don't you sit him down for a chat?"

Tina gets frustrated, she says "We've tried that: but Peter gets all high and mighty: then Kevin clams up, won't admit to anything," she grimaces. "Then he does that thing with his eyes, he knows I hate."; I'm constantly amazed that she's my daughter; Why doesn't she look for books on handling stroppy kids in the library? Why not do what I do, there's always advice on the web - or she could even ask someone who she feels he might confide in to talk over his problems.

"Would you?" Tina smiles, "Talk to him, you're so much better at that sort of thing."; Somehow I managed to walk straight into that one...

***

119

When I see Kevin again he's outside Woolworths, and his mates are teaching him how to swear, so I decide that I'll keep my distance - it's a male bonding thing, he's not very good at it and they're all laughing when I turn up.

"Hello Gran," he blushes upon seeing me, removing a cigarette from his mouth and trying to stamp it out before I've seen it.

"What brand are they?" I glare at him. He tries to explain that when it comes to smoking he can take it or leave it. He thinks he looks so mature leaning against the bin with his muddy trainers; vice grip jeans and black T shirt. Later, he arrives at my doorstep - he tries to assure me that despite what his Mum's implied he isn't doing drugs.

"Mum has no right searching through my room," he's angry.

"She's worried about you..." I point out, and he reluctantly accepts that: and promises he'll talk with her about it.

***

Well, having talked for a while, Kevin agrees to talk to his Mum. It isn't long before he's spending less time with his 'gang' and starting driving lessons. That's when he tells me about Tanya, this girl he's met - next thing I know he's got his' L' plates. Anyway: he says, if I see her around I can wave if I like: but not make him too nervous, he says. Tanya's been teaching him how to drive so I admire her already - Kevin's mother was very difficult to teach: because she's one of those drivers who's convinced she knows everything.

***

So, I come back from my holiday and I'm astounded, there's
Kevin and he's waiting for me at the late night shopping centre: parked on the kerb, waiting for me .

Loaded down with shopping, I dash towards the car.

"Oh, you're a good boy!"Kevin just grimaces at me. I notice

the breasts in the passenger seat "I don't believe we've been introduced."

"-This is Tan, she's been giving me some driving lessons." Kevin introduces me to this stunning red-head.

"Is that what they're calling it now?" Tan winks back at him, and he blushes.

"Nice to meet you dear!" I squashed into the back seat. I later learned that her name was Tanya and they'd met outside Woolies that Wednesday, they'd been dating for a while: but Kevin wasn't ready to introduce her to his family yet: he wanted to get engaged: but Tanya was going off him in a big way because she didn't want to be owned by anyone, and he smelt like an ashtray.

"He's a difficult person to teach, never in the same car twice!" Tanya adds sarcastically. "Where's the other one, again?"

"-Being repaired..."

"-So , he says," ; Tanya tells Kevin off for taking his eyes off the road and starts to use some extremely graphic, though highly justified expletives when Kevin picks up speed: He's showing off, pumping that accelerator.

Just drop me off at home!" I instruct him, I have no wish to be the meat in this particular sandwich. Suddenly a siren wails, Kevin silently curses and Tanya screams that he should pull over.

"Is it an ambulance?" I frown back at them, trying to ease out of my seatbelt and squint behind her.

"No, it's the police," Tanya frowns, burying her head in her lap. She apparently has a bad feeling about this, she says that 'we' should have seen this coming.

"I wonder what they want?" I see their plastic coats, as they swagger towards us in the side mirror.

"They'll probably be wanting the car back!" Kevin suggests: and the air inside the car turns blue.

© 2001/2002

121

GIFT FROM "GOD " STORIES

Some stories just write themselves or can gel together really easily, two of three of these tales Passengers, Brainstorm and Worst-Case Scenario were based on notes made on bus journeys.

Some stories are loosely based on real-life events. Camping Trip for example on my nephew's idea to tie a balloon to a tent to identify it, some can even come to you in dreams and need a gentle hand in the edit to make them acceptable for publication and No Dreams Allowed fits that category.

You'll remember that some of the fantasy titles had issues with 'tone'
well, both No Dreams and Brainstorm had similar issues firstly how to describe the images of Claire's dream among taste concerns and Brainstorm had a whole sequence relating to driving – for this collection I've returned to my longer edits and varied the content a little the condoms are back, replacing elastic bands and the 'B' word is used once in context - sorry if this offends you but I feel the audience here ,is a little different from the Coffee Break Pages.

A word about titles – sometimes they take a little while to develop, No Dreams was offered as 'Happy New Year' and I doubt anyone would have minded Stormy Morning; but how about Idylic Idols, Camping Trip was due to be offered in Australia as 'There'll Probably Be Spiders'.

Incidentally, please notice the commas around the word god, it's not a good idea to offend on religious grounds. I did briefly consider reworking 'Passengers' for 'The People's Friend' as 'The Long Autumn of Love' but I just couldn't get it to work – oh and if a magazine wants stories that are "all lengths, all styles" then 1,000 or 2,000 words are probably best..

No Dreams Allowed

Of course, I rang my client advisor the minute that I could muster up the courage, I told him about the interview and how it would of course be inappropriate to take the position - and he, bless him arranged for me to go and meet Adam and his er, "supervisor" to discuss my grievances.

'I'm shocked.' Adam's sighing at me, 'we had such a nice chat, you'd met us all, you seemed very keen, ticked all the right boxes.' Sandra's nodding in agreement; Sandra is Adam's Supervisor - today's the first chance I have to read her name badge.

'Yes, that's right..'

'So, was it something, I said or did, that made you change your mind?'

'No,' I'm shaking my head, 'not exactly..' I don't know how to begin, 'you know how I talked about my "ex"?'

'You called him a pig.' Adam's even noted that down on his notes from the interview.

'That's right.' I glance down seeing my reflection in the cream table, 'and he is! And you were very nice to me by comparison..' I glance across at what they call the "Safety Zone"; the plastic balls; the slides - for the moment they're vacant - and good thing too!

If I'd accepted this job I'd have been serving coffees to relaxing parents over the other side of the room - and quivering with fear whenever I saw Adam and recalled what had happened last night..

'So why not come and work for us?' Sandra's smiling at me.

I certainly need the money - since the pig walked out on me with the Council Tax and the colour telly. 'But, it wouldn't be right..'

Adam sighs, 'This is difficult,' he explains, 'Job Centre Plus have said that you might loose money if you can't give them a good reason, and we don't want to see that happen.' He shakes
his head. 'Claire, we like you..'

'It, wouldn't be the training, would it?' Sandra glimpses at my file. 'Sometimes, the fear of having that responsibility with First Aid, the

123

course is very thorough and, we'd keep a close eye on you..'

'No it's not the training,' I quiver.

Adam starts to change tact, 'Sandra you know procedure,' he pulls up his seat, addressing me more softly after he's done so, 'perhaps Claire, you'd like to talk to Sandra about anything I've done.' He gulps, 'Sandra, you're going to have to follow procedure, where I'm concerned,' Adam starts to walk away.

Sandra leans forward, she wants to hold my hand, but she brushes it, 'Adam requires me to ask you if he might have done something, did he perhaps? Did he, brush against you or suggest inappropriateness at the interview..' She asks.

In the minutes that follow she's explained that although they've arranged the meeting to clear the air and work out a solution, her only course of action where Adam is concerned, is to suspend him from duty.

'No,' I can't believe she's going to take it this far, 'it's nothing he did, I don't

want him suspended.' I'm trembling as I speak, and I'm going red, all blushing. 'Really, it's me, I don't think it would be right to work here with kiddies after..'

Sandra smiles, 'You did mention, and I hope you won't mind me pointing it out, that you and your husband have been trying for children of your own..'

'That's right, and it would just upset me to work here..'

'You'd be in the café.' Adam edges back to the table and sits back down. He had explained what my role would involve on that Friday; emptying the dishwasher; cleaning up - and it was not that I didn't adore small children especially - and come to think of it that was ironic; my husband, you see had blamed me for years, so how ironic that our problem had been in his department so to speak; and doubly ironic that I'd be swapping our kitchen there for their kitchen here.

'Claire,' Sandra urges, 'I feel we should be bringing in someone more neutral to discuss all this,' she jangles her finger in front of

me - it's an engagement ring. 'I should have said that Adam and I are quite close, so although I'd like to clear this up reasonably today that would be fine, if not Adam's agreed he should be suspended, while we launch an official inquiry..'

'-And, I wouldn't be able to continue working here if there was even a glimmer of a chance I'd been, inappropriate.'

'An official inquiry?' I gasp. I never wanted that; I can't believe this is happening; this is so bloody unfair. But this is their small business; they love each other; love working together: you can see it on their faces, and to save "him" I have to betray myself. 'He didn't touch me inappropriately,' I want to yell, 'you don't have to call in the Police, he isn't a danger to the kiddies, only I'm less of a lady,' I'm taking a deep breath, 'you see on Friday Night after the interview I went home and dreamed about him..'

Sandra's frowning, 'You dreamt, about my Adam?'

'Yes,' I look away, 'we were - in there,' I point to the slide and the Safety Zone with its catchment of plastic balls, only we were, busy!' I close my eyes, 'I hate myself! I must be going mad or, anyways, don't you see? I can't work with him - if..' I look up finally and Adam is blushing profusely; he'd been so nice.

'Sandra, I never..'

Sandra takes a long hard look at the safety zone; she's clearly thinking what a nutter I am - then she doing the most incredible thing - she's laughing, with relief it seems, she can't control her merriment; and she's making me feel about this high..

'Claire?' She asks me at last, 'Are you saying that you dreamt you were being intimate with my, future husband - and that means you need help?'

'Well, doesn't that mean that I, fancy him?' I gulp, 'I mean, I'll

be honest, it scared me, not that he wasn't...I can't work with him.'

Adam is totally stunned, 'All I said was "Please" and "thank you".' He's saying, 'I didn't, we didn't..' He frowns, 'I'm curious you say we were in the play area..'

'That's right..'

'And, you'd have seen pretty much everything, my bronzed tan, the tattoo on my left shoulder.'

Sandra notes my frown, she seems encouraged by this, 'It's just a dream,' she

smiles at me, 'being intimate, that can mean a new start - can I ask you a very personal question?'

'If you must.' I prepare myself.

125

'When you and your ex were trying for a baby - did it all get stressful, anxious, mechanical..'

'Well,' I nod, 'it did, yes.'; He said that having children now was me dreaming and they'd be no dreams allowed.

'We've been there,' Adam and Sandra nod knowingly. 'So Sandra, you're big on symbolism in dreams, help the young lady out..'

'Were there children in the dream?'

'No!' I puzzle, 'I don't think so,' I'm confused.

'Well it probably means that there's something new on the horizon - and that you have to be less serious with yourself - and learn to have, fun,' she hesitates, 'and this is the perfect place for that..'

'What?' I glare at them. 'You'd still like me to work here, even though...'

Sandra nods. 'I'm glad you came in to sort this all out with us,' she pauses, 'starting a new job can be quite daunting.'

Adam nods in agreement with her. 'Just remember we only want you to serve coffees, light lunches. We're not expecting you to do it topless.'

'Adam!' Sandra lightly punches his arm, and then I suppose we shake on it. A while later Sandra stops me by the Coke machine. 'You know I'm secretly rather envious.'

'Oh, yes?'

She nods, 'I only ever get to dream about George Clooney!'

***

'Claire!' Adam's come in with a big grin and nearly knocks the dishcloth out of my hand. 'Thank-you!' He breezes in.

'Oh that's all-right,' I frown, 'what for?'

'-For being so honest with us!'

'Oh?'

'That night, Sandra and I,' he pauses to clear a tray away.'We had a really long chat.' He wipes ketchup from his cuff. '-About, why, she hadn't felt threatened by you, symbolism and stuff?'

126

'Oh right?' I'm studying the clock on the wall while cleaning one of the laminated menu cards.

'I asked her what it meant that we both worked in a Children's Play business, and she said, it could just be co-incidence or it might mean, we feel insecure..'

'Insecure?' I frown.

'Then, we talked about our dreams, what we hope and dread about the future - all our insecurities, you know how your husband and all that..' Adam finally manages to catch his breath, 'So, I booked into this well man clinic and I've got the all clear..'

'That's fantastic!' I'm still trying to sound enthusiastic about it, when he asks me.

'Sandra..' he breathes in, 'Well, she wants to know would you like to manage the place while we're both on leave?'

'On leave?'

'You know, maternity and paternity leave?'

New horizons; new challenges, new beginnings - and promise for the future, sure: but how come they're off having all the fun - while I'm doing all the hard work?

© 2005

notes: There are rules about sexual imagery in short story magazines and it gets very complicated when the themes are adult in nature, in the case of "No Dreams Allowed" inappropriate behaviour has consequences that are quite heavy so it needed a legality edit and was offered later as "Happy New Year"

The following story "Brainstorm" even had problems with its title – it is offensive to those that suffer epileptic conditions, however, I've retained it here as it clearly describes the effect of post exam mind-cramming mixed with puberty; in this case, I'm reminded of the BBC guidance that love scenes should be romantic rather than sexual in nature before the watershed, which seems good advice for a family magazine – but for this edit I've prepared a fair compromise between the versions I offered.

127

Brainstorm

There's a satisfying crackle when you're walking through an autumn forest - it's true that it wasn't quite autumn the first time Kevin and I first done it - and it was colder, much colder than it ever should have been. The weather was changing so suddenly that we almost missed it: and it wasn't just a change in the weather; we changed forever that day.

A change in the weather. The sky darkens like all around - then little pellets of ice targeted us like pigeon droppings; and we were never going to get to sanctuary fast enough.

I recall that when I looked up, Kevin and my dog, Rex were both looking worried; it felt close and clammy - like any moment my world was gonna end. Then I heard the sky ignite in grey beckoning.

And, I say to Kevin: "There's a storm coming."

He cuddles me closer - close enough to smell my freshly conditioned hair.

'Rex!' Rex is straying on his leash - as in seconds the ground turns to sloppiness, all I can hear is the sound from the sky. Rex is straining; tugging; pulling - and I think for one awful second he's going to tear my arm off. I'm skidding, and I know things are going to get messy: but Kevin runs and splashes and grabs me and we slide together, sloppy - wet, and sloppy; it's all so sloppy.

I can remember shoving my bus money into my jeans; it had been all warm and clammy in my hand and I can still recall the sound it made as it rolled across his wooden floorboards - that was so embarrassing; we had decided to split up while I finished my exams, strange, I never thought we'd go through with it...

***

They've been looking at each other - and she thinks I haven't noticed. When she knows I'm watching she goes all distant and cold - but then I see that glance that passes on her face,

And, I go cold: I know that look so well - and he pulls her forwards; and I see how much she's been enjoying their kiss, and they hear the sound of my choking engine as I pull into a skid - there's only one person that's going to be parking around here!

***

'We're not going to be seeing each other for a while..' She announces, and that's what made me recall, a special moment with Kevin. Jessica sounds very mature: but I've had my deja-vued.

'So I saw..' I can't help blushing, as she fumbles through her bag.

'Well, I have to make sure he doesn't forget me.' She zips up her bag. 'It was just a snog!' She objects, 'You snogged Dad before you married him didn't you?'

'-Oh-yes..' I can see my smile in the right-hand mirror. 'A couple of times..'

'How did you do on biology Mum?' Jessica really wants to know.

'I aced it..' I recall - that's why I'm there and she's here. 'A month apart,' I nod, 'it's worth it.'

'We think so,' Jessica nods. 'Stewart respects me far too much to blow my exams.' ; I love the way she speaks for him in our conversations; she makes him sound far too understanding for my liking.

Of course when that month is up they can do anything they like - they know and I know it; things might develop far too quickly that's my worry - like mother, like...

So, they're going through this 'separation' - it's obviously Jessica's idea and although I hope I didn't push her towards it.

'You have a firm head on your shoulders my girl..' I'm choked: it takes a long time to learn to care for another person like that.

She nods. 'Can we still text?' She frowns, 'I don't know if that's

129

still dating or what?'

'Of course you can text!' I smile back as we pull away from the kerb. 'You can write to him too, as long as you don't use your right hand..'

'Oh,' she pauses, 'Oh it's okay. I think Stewart's pretty much ambidextrous..'

'-Jessica!'

She smiles back, cheekily.

I feel really sad for them: I feel like I've pushed them apart; love has to be responsible: but it shouldn't be their straight jacket; I might be really blinkered for a mum but I'd rather that they were kissing and cuddling than being texted to death; I'm curious how long will they last before they take things to the next level and how far up it is these days? You know, the fluffy slippers and tingling toes?; Like her father and me - I wonder if like us they'll have their own pair of toothbrushes. Kevin didn't know how to hold it.

'You hold a lady around the waist..' I recall touchingly - it's what I've always told him - what it seems I'll be telling him all our lives.

***

Outside the sky is purple and threatening, we splash along - laughing now - we're soaked! It's too late to be taking this seriously, Rex steps straight in and starts shaking himself all over the floorboards.

'Sorry..' I mouth.

'What's a wet dog supposed to do?' He smiles - and I find that I just have to kiss him.

'You're soaked!' We're just dripping all over each other. 'Why don't you go up and dry off?' He pauses, 'You can borrow one of my shirts if you like..'; And his shirts - they smell of him don't they? I'm hesitating inhaling his fragrances, before I quaver. 'I'm sure Mum won't mind you borrowing some trousers..' He summarises, following

me up the stairs. 'You're going to have to hurry if you want to catch that bus.'

As I wander back into their lounge, I look out at the rain-soaked windows; it feels threatening - inside, it's safe and warm, cosy - I feel cosy that's the word, hailstones splinter on the windows: and I recall it's so dark I can hardly see anything more than that worried look in his eyes: that horrified wonderment at my change of plans; the first he really knew was when I kissed him.

He lingers, unsure. 'You'll be late, your dad will kill me..' He's hesitating.

'Tragic,' I gulp, 'I want to be with you..' I whisper, 'Where we'll be safe..' And our fears, they melt away..

*

'So, I can text him?'

'Yes.'

'If I send him an E mail, is it okay to call him-' she starts watching all the parents and toddlers walking past.

'What?' I frown, and she leans forward and whispers. 'If you can spell it, you can send it - long as, I don't have to proof read it and you don't accidentally send it to my boss, again.'

'Sorry about that..'

***

'Mum..' She's helping me in with a cardboard box full of groceries which she puts down on the table. She's going to ask me a question, and she's sounding all embarrassed.

'Jessica?'

'When did you know, when it was right for you to, become more, you know. ?'

'More intimate?'

She nods; "More intimate" that's very bashful for her: when you think she's been revising with 'him' at that table - I've heard her revising for Science, all those medical terms - now she's being coy.

131

'You just know,' I blink, reaching to fill up the kettle, 'when it's right for you, don't rush these things.'

'Right,' she nods, 'that's what I said..' She frowns, 'How did you fill your time while you were waiting for your results?'

'I didn't do my last exam!' I blurt out - and the air is wounded, Jessica's shocked at first. 'I knew I wouldn't have passed it. And the weather was awful: but, inside I felt, safe.'

'What did you do instead?' Jessica smiles, 'Dad says, you were with him..'

'We, we did a, jigsaw,' I recall hazily, 'that summer we got very good at, doing jigsaws..'

Jessica seems satisfied: but I wonder if she knows, if she's worked out that it was nearly nine months before we discovered that we'd put all those pieces in the right places. Why do those first tender steps of my love life, once, so passionate and exploring, now seem to have become so downright sleazy?

***

I know they've moved beyond the zest of simply kissing.

Jessica seems so closed today, lost in her thoughts. She's probably thinking about him: but it's great that they're so happy. poor little thing; sometimes, she's, only closed to me - mind you, sometimes I prefer that.

'Jessica, you know what we were talking about the other day?'

'She nods.

'When I said: "You just know when it's right.."?: well, sometimes that just isn't true. Sometimes all those feelings get confused: and, I won't regret for one minute what, we created that summer: it wasn't the most intelligent thing I ever did..'

'Mum?'

'Jessica, you have put your seatbelt on, haven't you?'

She frowns, tapping it.

'And, Jessica, when Stewart takes you driving, he does wear his seatbelt, doesn't he?'

She looks bewildered.

'That's good because, Stewart might not be as safe, a driver as I

132

am, he might want to accelerate too quickly. Whenever you feel it's 'right' a seatbelt is very important to keep you both protected.'

'I'll make sure he's, always wearing one..' She nods. .

It's a gorgeous day. Jessica's last exam and I've arrived just in time to wait and collect her - and then I see Stewart hovering at the bus stop.

'Mrs Mathews,' he smiles at me.

'Paula please.' I smile.

'Paula,' he hovers, 'Jessica text to say she has this terrible headache so she might finish early..' He explains.

It's so hot. I can feel the sun cream melting on my forehead. I scan the road ahead. Sure enough, I can see her drifting out and looking about. I smile back to Stewart.

'Well, why don't you pop over for a celebratory dinner this evening?'

'I'm not sure,' he frowns, 'I think Jessica's got plans.'

I nod. 'Well, we'll see about it later then..' I nod before driving off in pursuit.

'Mum?' Jessica's looking around her - she's waiting for Stewart, 'Are you all right?'

'I'm fine dear..' I reassure her, 'How's your head?' I ask sniffing in some sun cream, and rubbing at my eye.

'Have you seen Stewart?' She asks.

I nod. 'Why don't you give him a ring later?'

She pauses, it's obvious just by that watchful hopefulness that's painted on her face.

'Come on Jessica...' I smile, opening the passenger door seat, 'I'll give you a lift.' I massage some sun cream back into my nose and rub stained hands across my skirt. 'It's no wonder you're feeling a bit heady. I can feel a storm coming..'

© 2005

133

Passengers

I remember the first time I saw him - it was on that kinda day where leather seats scorch your arms because it was so hot.

Mum and Dad had dragged 'our' land-rover, a clunking great thing that it was, into this sweet little car park that seemed to be stuck over a cliff; idyllic!

We were going to be walking up in the hills some-where: but you know what it's like - they both went off to find the toilets and there was I, yours truly, left to sit and think about how I had zero influence in the direction of my life. I decided to go on ahead, just for a peek...

I remember thinking how boring this was; how bored I felt: paths and stony walkways have never done it for me - I'm sorry: but I was pining for my big brother, Adam who was off with his girlfriend Gina getting to know her 'family' as it happened, but that's a funny story for another time that we'd be updated on upon our return.

Anyway, I was bored: nothing to do but count my freckles, suncream my moles and reason that me and walking just didn't get on; the hiking plimsolls had taught me that, and my poor scrunched up toes swimming in pussy goodness and sore spots - I really paint the picture well don't I?

So, I was forced to sit down - I just had to collect my thoughts together and take the weight off my toes. This thoughtful person had a bench planted in his honour - I think his name was Roger, hope he hadn't died hiking around here, well from where it was positioned, with a view of the valley across - that was a possibility.

So I'm edging forward, and peering over the barrier, I can see all these people trundling down the next slope below the sheer drop.

'Hi!' I call down - and, they're ignoring me, so I call again, because I hate that: I don't like being ignored, a few old dears look up at me, wondering where the noise is coming from, some even look up and smile in my direction; well I won't say while adjusting their hearings aids because that's rude and I'm not a walking cliché .

So, most of them don't see me, am I surprised? No, because unless you're rolling around testing Gina's mattress with Gina, holidays make you invisible; it's a puberty thing; they also make you deaf too: or so it seemed recalling the previous night, when certain close relatives, I thought were well past it thought I was asleep; let's not go there please - let's put all that lust down to the outpouring of Malibu and Orange and dream fondly of (TOPICAL MALE HUNK).

Well, as I looked down, I saw this clutch of blazers, so I cup my hands together, to make a funnel :and I yell down another greeting: but there is only one boy that even looks as if he can see me, although he's trying to ignore me - by talking with his mates.

'Hello!' I call, and my arm waggles - and as he looks up at me, by craning his neck, my bracelet simultaneously hurls from my wrist to my knuckles - and I don't try to stop it - because he's smiling up at me: and this is all part of our mating game - and today I'm feeling hot! I stand on the seat to look closer.

'Hi!' He smiles back.

And, I'm amazed that my heart is still beating - and I lunge, slipping forward to grab at my bracelet, I straddle, I grope and I slump - and my bracelet flies over the safety barrier - and goes all the way over the top - and I slither! Straight off the seat and onto the one patch of wet earth in this entire universe. I slither on a patch of wet grassy slope, falling plimsoll over freckles - I fall on my face, fortunately 'cause at least it would hide my blushes.

***

Mum helps me up, and so me and the old's make it down the hill and it's the hottest part of the day - so we're all sitting under the shades, pergola thingies.

I've decided by now that I'm happier being a mega geek - besides I've lost him - there's no way he's going to look for me after seeing how I fell for him. By now, Mum's found my headphones, so I can sit in complete oblivion..

When..

'Hello again!'

135

I frown, removing my headphones; Adonis is smiling, so I place my headphones down on the table. Well, he's not blond, in fact he's a bit spiky; ask your Parents about Gareth Gates, you'll get my picture.

'I'm Owen..' He introduces himself and he leads me not quite by his hand to sit under his umbrella.

'Hello, I'm-" I smile, and see his eyes recalling something.

'I bet you'll never guess what I found..' And he peers across uneasilly at this aged gent who's smiling weirdly across at us - he's looking tired.

'What is it?' I ask Owen.

'Let's go and sit over the other-side..' He decides, and wouldn't you know it - as we start to feel all warm together the sun goes in and then the temperature drops and Owen's looking all pimply.

'I'm Becky..' I introduce myself. 'What have you found?'

'This!' He dangles, my torn bracelet.

'Where did you get it?'

It must have fallen from heaven, like you..' He smirks, 'That sounded so, corny!' We have a good laugh and watch everyone else eating around us: and finally, Owen offers me this sandwich and as I take my first bite - he tells me not to eat any more of it.

'Why?' I cough - and my eyes are watering. He glares back at his mates on the corner and then he peels it open and shows me the peppers. He hovers in his seat - I can feel my mouth starting to ulcer. Then, I hear the laughter from the table opposite, it begins and it just never seems to end.

'They told me to do it.' He apologises; it must be some initiation thing. And he's grinning and laughing back at his friends; and I'm so disappointed in him - until he looks back, and I realise his eyes aren't laughing. He tells me that there was no other way they'd let him sit with a girl, so I'll let it pass - especially as he lets me suck his seven up.

***

Mum and Dad never came over to see what all the laughter was

136

about - that is so typical! Owen might have been snogging me across the table and they wouldn't have budged; I've known them to have been more interested in the colour to repaint the downstairs toilet than in my love life. Thing is, that old guy strays over to our table and stares at me.

'Have you given it to her yet?' He asks and Owen takes him to one side.Owen glares him out and he backs off back to his seat.

'What was that all about?' I want to know.

'Nothing really..' Owen ponders, 'Well if you must know he wants to know if I've, kissed you..'

'-Poor guy!'

'Yeah,' Owen doesn't know what to say, 'sad.' He sighs into his lunch-box.'You, look cold.' He says at last and wraps my perspiring chest in his blazer.

'Thank you!' I deflate, 'So are you on a trip with your school?'

'Might-be!' Owen becomes coy, then notices I'm smiling. He grimaces, 'It's that obvious?'

'You're wearing your school uniform!' I reply dryly.

'Oh yeah!' I think for one fearful exacting second that he's going to touch me. 'Well you tend to forget.'

'You must be hot..' I smile, and he backs off. 'Where are you going?' I start to babble, 'I mean what school are you from?' I ask all interested: but my brain's thinking; *do you want to kiss me, because I wouldn't mind.*

'-Nowhere you'd know..'

'-Sorry?'

He's scowling, 'We tend to get isolated..' He glares across at his friends. 'Neanderthals!' He hisses.

I respond with something that sounds like: "You'll be welcome in my cave any-time," but it doesn't come out as clear as that once I'd realised how wet that was going to sound.

'I'm sorry about the peppers.' He takes back his blazer.

***

Owen's back five minutes later, I've sat drooling while he's returned to say he can choose his own friends and he wants to sit

137

with me - and who am I to argue?

'How are you doing love?' Mum voice rears up nervously behind us.

'Fine,' I smile at her and feel my back ping where it straightened so fast. 'This is Owen. He's here with his school.'

'Oh that's nice dear..' Mother doesn't think, 'Dad and I are over by the fountain. We were hoping, perhaps you'd come and join us.' She bends closer. 'Owen, I'm sure you're a nice young man, but Becky is supposed to be spending time with us..'

'Mum!' I growl: but the moment is ruined. Why don't I just crawl under the parasol and stay there? One moment ago, I was admiring Owen, and I was looking into his eyes, and we were canoodling; and I was wearing this beautiful dress and the aisles were swaying. Now, I'm stuck in Sixth Form, watching frogs "do it" and pinging condoms at my fellow inmates; with mum around it's all cold, scientific - and distinctly unromantic.

'I have to go...' I say, scrawling my phone number on a paper hanky - and I think that for one god awful moment that he's going to kiss me - I mean how embarrassing would that have been in front of Mum? *Well, she's looked away now so you can if you like - and if your cold little paw should accidentally brush that pickle off my breast - well, we'd be the only ones to ever know - apart from the security camera and the thousands of gawping puritans and..Hey! Mr Suave have I vanished again because you didn't seem to miss me when you glued your eyes to my chest..*

I brush his hand away because plainly, I'm not interested.

'Can, I have your E mail address?'

'-Why?'

'Then we can E mail each other.' He points out.

'OK..' I whisper shyly, realising that I've just fallen in love twice with the same guy.

'Take care Becky.' He drools. Notice, I didn't give him my E mail address - a girl likes to play hard to get: and then I go cold; Looking back at my table where I'd put down my headphones; I feel empty like the table - and I see him laughing and joking with all his mates - and he must see my crumpled little face staring back at him - how could it have been so easy?

Was it worth it? I stare back. We could have had trust and intimacy I thought we were soul mates - and that bastard took my headphones ; I'm left reasoning how any day, now, he's gonna ring me up, and rub my nose in it - twenty quid ;he broke my heart for twenty quid.

'Has he gone love?' Mum places her hand on my shoulder.

'Yes,' I turn back to her, my eyes fuming. '-And the, swine took my headphones.' I glare, 'And, I really liked him. 'I hoped Mum hadn't heard that bit: but she's smiling much too knowingly for my liking.

'Oh, Becky dear, I don't think he did.' Mum places the headphones in front of my face, and I snatch at them before they disappear into oblivion. 'I thought they were a bit exposed so I took them off the table.'

'Oh mum!' I begin to explain all that's happened,'I thought it was fated. He found my bracelet, and there was no way he could have, I really liked him, but he's never going to ring me. '

'Why not?' Dad comes over - he must have heard everything I've just told Mum in confidence.

'He, probably thinks I've got a face like a pig.'

'I'm sure he doesn't,' Mum sighs.

'Did you give him your number?' Dad asks gently.

'Yes,' I gulp, 'I suppose I did..'

'Well there then,' Mum breathes in. 'He'll have to ring you back!' Dad agrees with her, he mumbles something about it being against the law for him not to - which was nice, for him.

'-Oh, excuse me love!' That familiar elderly gent is walking over to us, a woman walking with him wants to ask me something.

'Yes, what is it?'

'Did that nice young man give you back the bracelet I found?'

'-You, found?' I peer into the sun. I step back flabbergasted; this can't be happening.

'Well Cedric found it,' the lady nods to her friend, the man Owen said was asking weird questions. 'Well I'll be honest, I was a little unsure to approach you, so Cedric gave it to the boy, we thought it best, ah.' The lady can see Mum pointing to the bracelet on my arm.

'Thank you,' I smile back at them, 'I'm very grateful.' I don't

139

know why but I reach up give Cedric a peck on the cheek – because I reckoned he'd earned it; and I thought that Owen had treated us both shabbily.

They nod and walk away, leaving me thinking.

'Are you alright love?' Dad puzzles.

'Owen, he said: "It must have fallen from heaven," like me!' I shake my head, 'I must have fallen really hard!' I can't believe it, 'what a sleaze!'

Mum takes my hand as we walk into the shade, 'We all fall from heaven', she recalls cheerily. 'It's where we end up that's the important thing!' She later explains that I shouldn't be too hard on Owen for lying about how he got my bracelet back - all men exaggerate it seems - and she points out that destiny can sometimes be scary.

On the way back to the Car Park, Dad buys me an ice cream - and Mum promises to be a little more considerate in the future.

In return, I've decided to forgive each one of Owen's imperfections knowing that we were both just passengers on this journey we had no choice in - and no, I never did hear from Owen again, well that wasn't so surprising in my rush to avoid giving him my E mail address - I'd forgot to include the dialling code.

***

I'd have preferred to leave Owen in the past – you know my first love, my incomparable someone whom I could dream fondly of at 'romantic' moments? So how sad that someone had the bright idea of tracking him down – they rooted him up from Australia to reunite us.

My daughter's going to be five next week – and I was really looking forward to telling her about Owen, first love and how you get 'mushy' feelings: I'd have said that "You'll never forget your first love."

Now, she can watch the special DVD of our "reunion" where I recall our day together and he'll just look tiredly into my eyes as if he's just stepped off a plane after a long flight and he's wondering where the toilets are. The reconstruction is even better; they couldn't film at the same location – the car park was gone! Yes, we were surprised too – it suffered a landslide a few weeks after our visit – and it's filmed in Sepia with two supposed 'doubles' that make me rather envious – and in Owen's case? Well he looked okay if I'd been wearing rose-tinted specs.

What you didn't see on telly was the magic moment when we smooched and I ended up gagging on an aniseed balll Owen was chewing to mask his breath.

You see, sometimes love's journey will take you to many different locations and will pull you in numerous directions – and you won't want to go back.

© 2005

note: "Passengers" was an interesting story to prepare for its appearance here; it was expanded to add something to the end of the tale and some of the original dialogue between Owen and Becky was toned down – for the version here I felt it needed a fresh look – I've restored the reward kiss for Gerald but taken out some of Owen's comments returned to the magazine re-edit – I'm still not sure about that kiss though..

Worst-Case Scenario

"What have you done?" I asked her angrily, as my face creased with confusion; I just knew what had happened – the minute I saw that look on her face; and she let out this unearthly growl that resinated from deep within.

I was about to leave, for work you see – what does one do in those circumstances? Confront the murderer, I suppose..

"Anyway, She dropped it and it wiggled behind the freezer – and it was self-aware – and moving. Well then she scurried off to get her breakfast, and I realised I'd have to catch my bus.

"So I'm sat there with my drinking chocolate trying to put the scenes of torture to the back of my mind – and I thought.."

"What if it chews through the cables?" A voice replies dryly. "Which was when you rang me."

"That's right, yes." I recall that I've been talking far too long – even for a Customer Service phone line. "What I want to know is, are we ensured for 'Acts of Cat' I mean in the worst-case scenario?"

"Well, that depends, is he a big cat?"

"Domestic," my mood brightens. "Just a moggy."

"-Just a moggy.!" He repeats calmly, before clearing his throat "Well, did you take steps to prevent an incident occurring?" He wonders. "Did you close any doors to isolate the cables?"

"Well," I sigh, "I didn't really have time to think.." I recall, "It's her first victim you see: but she's desperately sorry – and she has Pet Insurance."

"-Oh,"

"-And a chip."

"-A chip?" I think I can now hear him sighing. "Well if you should get home and find that your house has been engulfed in a furball, um a fireball then please don't hesitate to put in a claim. Oh and one last thing," he pauses. "We do advise that you keep any important documents in a fire-proof box."

Fire-proof? That gives me another idea...

"No Miss, there have been no reports of any incidents at Ramwell Crescent..Fire? No, I don't think so.." I can hear mounting concern, until I explain further. "You think your Cat might have started a fire?" He sounds relieved, "Eh have you caught him playing with matches?" He asks – well there's obviously some interference on the line.

"A mouse?" He considers, "Or, it might be a rat.." He pauses. "But you think it's dead."

I can almost hear him nodding.

"-Can I ask, do you have a Residual Current Device, a surge protector?"

"-I don't think so, no."

"I see. Have you discussed with your other house-members what you'd do in the event of a fire?"

"Oh I don't know. Scream, I'd expect," I frown. "But my cat can use a ladder.

"There you are you see-you've thought of everything!" He cheers, "At least your cat can get out alive!" There's a brief hesitation – I think he's drumming his fingers. "I tell you what I'm going to do.." He explains, "You're obviously worried, so why don't you let me take down your details – and I'll send you a leaflet of simple fire safety measures.."; He sounded such a nice man – it was just the way he said 'simple'.

Well, by that point I had all kinds of visions in my head   - as you can imagine, so I reasoned that I'd just have to get someone to pop in and just check things out. My daughter Amanda, heard my concerns and offered to pop in during her lunch break, bless her.

"Oh, hello Mum," She breezes down the phone. It must be , oh two O' Clock before she deigned to ring me. "-I had to take Pickle to the vet.."

"What was the matter?" I ask her.

"Oh, nothing-really Mum. The poor little things had some painkillers and had her feet bandaged.."

"Goodness, what happened?" I wonder: my mind filling with visions of Pickle and an enlarged super-mutant in hurling, hissing

143

conflict. "Has, she been in a fight?"

"Well.."

"Amanda we agreed, if Pickle bought in rodents she'd have to go – vermin are a health-hazzard!"; That was my one condition for getting Pickle – how quickly Amanda's forgotten.

"Nothing like that Mum.." Amanda attempts to explain."You know that tree-support, the metal one in the garden?"

I nod, then remember she can't see me, "Yes," I grimace, "Was, there a bolt of lightening?"

"No," Amanda explains patiently, "Pickle used it as a scratching post."

"Really dear.." I don't believe her for a second. "-And, did you find the rat?"

"The rat?" She sounds bewildered, "Oh, the one down the back of the fridge?" She asks.; Fridge/ freezer what's the difference.

"Yes!"

"Oh, that was just an old leaf." She explains, "Honestly Mum I had more important things to worry about.."; And she does – She's helping out at the local stables, and the search for the cat-box has made her late.

"-'An old leaf." I sigh, "Well there's a relief.

Next day my next door neighbour is all smiles.

"Oh Millie dear!" She calls from over her garden gate. "That daughter of yours is a one.."

-"Amanda?"

"That's right," she nods, "She was out in your garden yesterday. The funniest thing I ever saw!" She recalls there was your cat walking with bandaged feet, looked a little poorly – but she was lucky Amanda thought it was a rat bite. She went to the vet apparently.."

"Yes, yes," I urge her – some people never get to the point do they?

"Well, I suppose she was trying to put the cat off from bringing you any-more trophies, said you didn't like it – but it's in their nature.." She explains the scene so eloquently, "There was this little cross, and a, a splattering of petals.."; My dear neighbour then

144

proceeds to splatter some imaginary petals with her hands – like we didn't already have enough on our patch. "It looked dashed odd!" She concludes, "And your poor little cat was looking very guilty.." She sighs, "But that was the thing – she showed me the corpse, it wasn't a rat."

"-It wasn't?"

"No, squidgy little nose – and little feet pointing into the air – it was, a mole!"

"A mole!" I'm delighted, poor weary Pickle can have a special treat tonight I promise her – I know, all god's creatures and all that but this, was a mole..

My deceitful daughter visited later that evening to take Pickle for her check-up.

"Oh hello dear!" I beamed at her; I might have let it go: but Amanda hadn't buried the mole very deeply and I was in a foul mood, so Pickle's special treat was off for the duration. You see – Pickle had dug up the mole's corpse and left it under the kitchen table – and now I could tell that it wasn't a mole at all; there is nothing little about moles – this was a shrew; as anyone can see when it's lying on your best carpet.

"Ah, yes.." I grimace, "I wanted to have a little word, about your leaf-burial!"

© 2006

notes: I had to leave for work on a Saturday morning and as I left our cat had bought in a 'rat' that was now hiding behind the fridge – I wrote "Worse-Case Scenario" on the bus to work, no-one was happier than me to see the shrews' corpse waiting on the kitchen carpet with our younger cat standing over it saying: 'It wasn't me..' but later a large mouse did get in and kill the boiler cable, on a serious note always check your gas boiler repair is carried out by someone with Gas Safe qualifications.

Two of the tales in this collection were previously inspired by my nephew Ben, who inspired the story of "CAMPING TRIP" and "THE LITTLE BOY IN THE MIRROR" there's a sequel to the next story which I wrote in my gap year, it was called "GOING TO A SPECIAL PLACE."

Camping Trip

'What's that?'Adam wants to know as I start to unfold his uncle's sleeping bag across the kitchen floor.

'It's a sleeping bag.' I explain, 'For Uncle Terry's camping trip.

'Oh,' he puzzles, his little mind is working overtime, I know they'll be more questions any minute. 'Won't it be very cold in their tent without any carpet?'

I grit my teeth, I've never really thought about it.' I smile.

'Perhaps we can lend them our little heater?' Adam suggests, then thinks on, 'no 'lecetric.' He sighs.

I hear Jenny coming down the stairs and see her pausing on the landing. She loves her new multi-coloured jumper - her gift from Terry, it suits her bubbly breezy personality - bright all right: it's ungracious I know, Jenny's lovely : but sometimes, I just want to hit her!

'What's the matter Adam?' She's studying my bewildered four year old.

'I think it might be too cold for Uncle Terry.' He considers, adding, 'Uncle Terry is really old!'

'Is he?' Jenny beams at me, 'Well he'll be really disappointed. Are you going to tell him?'

Adam goes very quiet, he's thinking it over. 'Alright..' He agrees, his loud little voice jarring up the stairs as he starts calling for Uncle Terry: but Jenny says she's got a better idea.

'I tell you what,' she suggests, watching me coyly, 'I'll stay really close to your uncle, and then our body heat will keep him warm.'

'Why?' Adam doesn't get it at all: and I'm left wondering how close to the edge Jenny's going to get; I've explained to him that Uncle Terry and Jenny are good friends and that they like each others company - and I think he understands - but Adam goes all silly when I try to suggest the new couple like 'each' other - he starts making spluttering noises. I blame his uncle: it was Terry that got him interested in spiders and cockroaches. Adam's always had a taste for the gothic - forget soppy things like love: if you want to get onto Adam's wavelength just talk to him about Tarantulas and you'll hold this four year old's attention for - well, for minutes really.

'So why are you staying in his tent? Adam ponders, 'Why not stay in a shall-'

' -A chalet?' Jenny suggests.

Adam nods.

' -Because, it's romantic!?' Jenny's eyes start to brighten and she's searching the ceiling.

'Doesn't sound very, mantic to me!' Adam considers, 'Sounds cold and creepy.' He grins mischievously. 'There'll probably be spiders!'

'Adam!' I glare across at him from the kitchen where I'm starting to unload cups from the dishwasher.

Jenny doesn't seem to mind taking the bait. 'Oh don't say that!' She fakes mock alarm.

'They'll probably want to crawl all over you..' Adam adds with a devious twinkle in his eye.

'Maybe Uncle Terry will save me?' Jenny suggests her voice tinged with melodrama, she's over-acting dreadfully.

'He's not very good in a -mergency.' Adam considers, 'Why do you want to go to a creepy old campsite anyway?'

'Well, they'll be playing music.'

'-In a field?' He sounds like he doesn't believe it: and it's hardly Terry's wisest decision, I must say.

'No,' Jenny frowns, 'well it will probably be in a field nearby.'

Adam's looking most concerned, he watches Jenny as she goes into the kitchen to help me collect together the cutlery.

'What's the matter darling?' I ask him. Jenny turns back to see his puzzled frown.

'What if it rains?'

'The tent's watertight.' Jenny smiles, mouthing "Well hopefully." In my direction.

'You can borrow an umbrella.' I suggest.

'I think it will be fine!' Jenny delights, then noticing Adam's frown she changes tack. 'But I will take it just in case.' She makes

148

sure Adam sees her putting in her case - and even lets him sit on the case to close it properly.

Adam still seems worried when all the packing has been done. 'What will you do if the batteries run out?' He asks.

'On the torch?' I smile back at Jenny's bewilderment.

'Oh,' Jenny clearly hasn't thought of that, she's still thinking, 'Does Terry have a compass?' She wonders.

Adam doesn't think so: but then he hops off his stool and dashes over to the food cupboard. We watch curiously as he takes out a strange multi-coloured bag and puts it on the table.

'Balloons?' Jenny seems delighted, she's wondering how they're going to help.

'You, aft- you put one on your tent, then you can see it across the field!'

'When it gets dark you mean?' Now Jenny's worked it out, 'You know, I think young Adam's a genius!' She congratulates me, brushing her hand through my little boy's hair in that way that annoys boys so much. She's still buzzing with enthusiasm when she explains it all to Terry - when he comes down from the bathroom.

***

It's starting to rain as they drive away. Terry's waving to us cheerily when Jenny spots Adam's worried little face on the way down the drive.

'What's the matter Adam?' Jenny dashes back to ask, Terry drifts beside her, wondering if they've left something behind.

'You will be careful not to fall over in the field won't you?'

'Of course!' Terry breezes.

'-No, I meant 'er..' Adam glares at Jenny.

'Er?' I frown at Adam.

'Jenny.' Adam explains, 'Uncle Terry doesn't have too much money.' There's a confused silence as I explain about the insurance ads on the television - sometimes you never know what a little boy will pick up.

'Oh,' Jenny smiles knowingly, 'then I'll be especially careful!'

149

Jenny promises as they say their farewells. 'Mustn't trip up, got it! Terry isn't very rich...' She looks back, smiling.

Later that evening Jenny texts me to say they're okay - and then they phone just that little bit too late for Adam's bedtime.

'Tell Adam, we haven't tripped up yet. We're being very careful.' Jenny's voice vibrates with the tones of the musical dirge behind them.

'Is that Aunty Jenny?' Adam rubs at his tired little eyes; it's obvious he's been worrying about them.

'Yes darling.' I assure him, 'No slip-ups.'

He smiles back, pleased they're safe.

Watching the weather forecast over those next couple of days I'm certain Jenny and Terry are having an interesting time - there's been nothing but constant deluges of rain; thunderstorms and hail mixed in with gentle soggy sunshine.

I phoned them once more, the next morning, just to pass on Adam's fraught concerns - he wanted to talk to them, something about the mud becoming like a bog - and that it would be like quicksand, Terry took it well - although the signal was weak, me? Well at first I was just concerned to know where he'd picked up a term like "bog" in our house, we say "toilet."

Well our two rain-soaked music fans drive back two days before the end of their holiday - strangely they're all smiles, like Adam when he sees them.

'It was rather dreadful!' Terry admits, as I clean the strands of straw and dry mud from off the table.

'Oh, I wouldn't say that!' Jenny thrusts her arm - or rather her hand into my face so I can study the gleaming object on her middle finger.

'After that first night and a half, we decided to book into a hotel.' Terry explains - while Adam soaks up his every word. '-But, we couldn't afford to stay there for very long...'

'-The two rooms, were quite expensive...' Jenny considerately

150

takes up the story, 'So, I said, it didn't matter about the concert I was happy with having his 'rhythms' in my life..' ; and if that sounds ever so slightly as damp as they were, it's because, I've ever so slightly censored what she implied by what she didn't quite say.

'-Then Terry proposed.'

'Why?' Adam frowns back at her, then studies Terry worriedly.

'Because, we, we love each other..'

Terry nods fishing out his boots from under the chair in the corner where they've been drying on a very old copy of The Sun.

'Oh.'

'-But what a holiday!' I bemoan, 'A complete washout!' I can hardly comprehend, 'You were trapped in your tent for how long?'

'About fifteen hours..' Jenny quickly re-admires her new jewellery.

'And it's pitch black, the batteries in the torch are dead..' They paint the picture so vividly.

'-And there's a slight drip from the roof..'

'Never!'

'Oh, I managed to fix it with some parcel tape.' Jenny assures me. Terry smiles back - and Adam looks so proud of his uncle - he's soon off in search of a screwdriver.

'The concert's rained off, the field's waterlogged, and it's pitch black.' I sigh, 'That's not my idea of romantic! I'm sorry.' Terry nods, then frowns in agreement - Adam's just returned to the kitchen table where he's trying to break the crust off Terry's hiking boots - with a screwdriver - Terry scowls at him, and strategically places his boots back under the chair out of harms way.

'I mean, what did you do all night?' I puzzle.

Jenny smiles cheekily, 'Well two young fit soon to be engaged people cuddling up to keep warm in the dark.'

I glow bright red, and Adam asks me why my face has gone that funny colour. Jenny's blushing.

Terry's grinning back at me. 'We were trying to decide what colour balloon to use, what else would we be doing?'

Adam studies his Uncle's face then looks at Jenny before scowling at me, and snatching back the screwdriver. 'Mummy, he loves her.' Adam smiles, then glares at Jenny. 'So, they're going to, go away and make lots of babies.'

Jenny, can't help but giggle at Terry, 'Well, one or two, one day..' She promises him. Adam goes very quiet and slips off to wash his hands.

When they've both dried out watching soaps in the sitting room, Adam asks me to go to the kitchen with him.

'I'm really going to miss Uncle Terry.' He sighs.

'What do you mean darling?' I think I know, Terry's engaged, so he'll be spending less time with his little nephew - and his big Sis; I'm going to miss him too. 'I'm sure he's going to visit and even if they move away, they'll stay in touch. We'll go and see them.'

'Yeah.' Adam considers, 'Not for long though.'

We watch as our two guests finish the washing up - they insisted, and then - we watch sadly as they leave a mountain of wet clothes on top of the tumble drier.

I've just finished hurling a very muddy copy of the Sun into the recycling bin when Adam attracts my attention.

'Mummy,' Adam grabs at my arm, 'Do you think I should remind Uncle Terry about what happens when they've finished mating?'

I gulp. Before I can muster any sort of response or figure out one zenith where my boy's mind is racing off to, I hear him calling me - from the back door.

'Oh no!' Adam's wailing as he watches them across the drive. 'She's started eating him already!'

notes: it can sometimes take a little time to work out how to end a story, the resolution to "CAMPING TRIP", like the next story took a while to work out but didn't need too many changes, "THE LAST STRAW" wasn't quite clear enough in the ending and was only finally completed after two magazines had rejected it.. I finally polished it for this collection...

The Last Straw

"I've been totally humiliated!" Susie's wailing at me.

"Oh, come on," I press her arm and look into her bewildered eyes, "I know it feels bad: but at least you know what he's like - and so what if he talked to her, about you?" I frown, "She won't judge you for it."

She pulls away from me. "He, told her private things about us." Susie shakes her head, "How I made impossible demands!"

"I'm stunned," I gulp, really I'm not stunned at all. "So what? You're well rid of him, if he wants to tell her your pillow talk, they deserve each other!"

"I still love 'im.." She sighs, resting her arm so that it lifts her chin.

"Oh you don't..." I despair, "You do.." ;This isn't good: Susie's never really loved anyone before - not like Stuart

"You've been with him three months," I hesitate, "but you can't let him use you, Suse, that's not love, not really." She hears what I'm saying: but I can see that she isn't really listening.

"I can't even bear to look at him." She hisses, "I'm upset, he's upset - but how did he expect me to react?" She despairs, "I never thought he'd treat me like that.."

"Well, if it's true you still love him, then you're going to have to talk.."

"Yes," She nods, "Only, I can't! That really was the last straw.." She growls, "He'll never understand how much he hurt me - he's put me in an impossible position!"

"-So you can't just forgive and forget?"

"No!" .

"Well no-one's asking you to, but is what he did really so terrible?"

"Not to you!" Susie glares, "You'd probably just pretend it never happened.." ; I hate that - how she demeans me like that, because I'm the 'boring' one that never has any 'fun'.

"If you must know, I wouldn't have slept with him until there

153

was a trust between us. I'd make him sleep on the sofa.."

"Right," Susie glares, "Well, I did trust him, he was going to move in with me." She looks wistfully up at the cream-coloured ceiling. "I thought we were happy.."

"-So, he was talking with her all the time you were together?"

"That's right!"

"-Plotting behind your back, spreading intimate gossip about your lousy love life, and how boring it was..."

"He's the one that makes it boring!" Susie growls, "I try to keep things interesting, I was given this book - and he just throws it back in my face by discussing all my failings.."

"No wonder you're angry!"

"We might not have had the most perfect relationship.."

I agree.

"-But I deserved better than that.."

"I'd be furious too!" I'm fuming, "What gives him the right to talk about you behind your back? With her of all people.." I'm thinking on my feet when it occurs to me, "Still.." I say.

Still what?" Susie frowns. She tries to grab my wrist and pull me back to the chair. "Still waters run deep? It's always the quiet ones? What do you mean?"

"Still, he came clean almost immediately,"

"After how long?" Susie sounds exasperated, "I'm sorry, but how can I take him back now?"

I agree. "I tell you what Suse, I'm gonna do something special just for you," I half smile, "I'm gonna go next door and thump him!"

Susie grimaces, "And, what will that achieve?" She's desperate, she lunges for me.

"It will make my best friend feel better," I grimace, "and it will wipe that self contented smugness clean off his face.."

"No wait," She pulls me back, "I want to speak to him.."

I thought she would.

***

"So," I hesitate inside the cafeteria, where it seems Susie and Stuart can't keep their hands off each other; several of their positions at the centre table are banned for health and safety reasons - and they're contentedly chewing each other's chins.

"What happened to you two last night?" I hesitate to come between them. "Let me guess. Stu made his big puppy dog eyes and you forgave him?" I despair at her sometimes.

"No," She smiles, "We had a talk about how he acted," Susie recalls, "and, well it was very cold last night and I decided he'd been punished enough." They kiss again, hungrily and I feel my stomach looping, I'm really happy for them - but don't tell them that will you?

"I don't want to hear it," I turn away, then I'm intrigued, "So what next?" I wonder.

"Oh that's already happened!" Susie informs me, as Stuart backs off to give us both some oxygen. "First thing this morning I went to see you know who..."

"You never!" I gasp.

Susie nods, "I told her that despite all her interference we were still rock solid." She smiles evilly, "I said, 'You must be able to still smell him on me, it was so early." She frowns, "I suppose that was a bit cruel.."

"I suppose, she had to be told.." I sigh, taking the warm seat opposite her. "What did she say?"

"Oh, that I'd got the wrong end of the stick and that she'd only got involved because Stuart was so easy for me to manipulate, because I had more experience."

"I'd say, lot's more." I see Susie glowering in my direction, so I shut up swiftly.

"Well," Susie grins, "I said that Stuart's matured considerably since he was last in her clutches, and if she wants to split us up, she'll have a fight on her hands - because I still love him - and that we were 'together' for most of last night, making, up for lost time."

"-For most of last night?"

"-Until he fell asleep in the bath.."

"Right." I smile.

"She said, I'd got her all wrong: that Stuart would soon realise his mistake - when I moved on to my next conquest!"

"-She said that, what a cow!"

"Can you believe that?" Susie despairs, "I've made an enemy for life.." She sighs, "So I was about to leave when I decided to explain that anything Stuart tells her about us must remain private from now on.." Susie grimaces, "And then, we hugged.."

"You, hugged her?" I'm dismayed, "Why?"

"Because, well she loves him too, and she's been a big part of his life for so long,"

"So, does she get an invite to your wedding?"

Susie nods, "Of course she does..."

"-But she tried to split you both up!"

"Yes, sad isn't it, how some people just can't let go?"

"So, after the wedding are you going to suggest moving in with your Mum?"

"Oh absolutely!" Susie smiles, "Mum's always wanted lot's of grandchildren - and I can talk to her about anything and she's never embarrassed to offer advice."

"So there's never any pressure?" I envy her - all the way to the drink dispenser at the edge of the room.

"Perfect isn't it?" Susie pops in a twenty pence and types in a number.

"-And she's always said that although she wouldn't want to influence me in any way, she's always thought the world of Stuart.."

"So, what about the er, other woman in Stuart's life?"

"Oh I think it scared her that he's in a healthy relationship. Once she's seen us at the altar she might finally get the message."

"You, think?"

"I'll just have to bite my tongue,"Susie sighs, "-Because she has a right to be there! It's not her fault," Susie considers it. "Stuart may have a gob like a leaky tap - but you have to make an effort with your future Mother in law don't you?"

notes: This was a story with a difference in that the story idea was just very witty dialogue, but the twist took a couple of years to make clearer to the reader – some stories only ever get sent out once or evolve into a more complex tale.

SEASONAL SAGAS

There are certain seasons of the year that everyone aims to write for – Christmas and Easter and Valentines Day all of these were offered and adjusted slightly – so here are some seasonal tales with a difference...

In 2006 I decided to take a gap year to work on longer projects; I'd been feeling that the short story women's magazine market was a nut I was never going to crack and I'd settled into finishing a novel and sending material overseas.

In March 2006, I injured my hand at work; at the time, I'd been working on a story called "EX DISPLAY" in long hand and by the time I was able to type again the markets were considering stories for Christmas - so I took this group of character's and reworked the idea; I added some Christmas shopping and thus, a story of a wife's deadly revenge was given a softer edge and seems sexier in this season of goodwill and forgiveness, despite the loss of the original love scenes from the US version – and it now covers other stronger emotive pitches and themes...

Collision Course

'Did anyone see what happened?' I ask, looking around hopefully: I was first on the scene - and what a scene; crushed shopping bags and tinsel, mixed with squashed turkey and crumbling sausage rolls; there's a broken bottle of alcohol free champagne and torn Christmas wrapping litters the crossing.

'He was moving so fast, I don't think he even saw her!' A lady in a brown fur hat and matching coat is sighing beside me.

'Has anyone called an ambulance?' I ask, crawling through the festive debris on bended knees while the carol singers in the square somewhere to the left search for their mobiles.

'Yes dear..' The lady assures me, as I reach the casualty, 'I said it was a hit and run..'

'I've got a pulse!' I smile up amongst the rabble of onlookers, there's a face concealed in the several layers of winter fluff, 'Can you hear me?' I ask loudly.

'My head hurts,' she moans, 'I want Chris..' She gasps, her face whitening before my eyes.

I turn back to the crowd, to where the lady in brown is getting help putting a shopping bag under the casualties feet - when I stare questioningly back I get a comment: "Face is pale, raise the tail.." And I'm not going to argue.

The casualty is looking distant.

'Tell me about Chris!'

'Chris is wonderful,' she smiles painfully, 'he's amazing!' She groans, 'He's bought me an engagement ring, I shouldn't even know, ouch!'

Looking down the length of her body, I see one of the onlookers is trying to ram my casualties shoe back on - I growl at him and he retreats, taking her shoe with him. 'It's really important that we don't move her. The ambulance will have special equipment for carrying..' It's just dawned on me, I don't know her name - and I'm curious.

'Charlotte,' she smiles bravely, squeezing on my cold hand. 'Try not to panic love,' I try to make my voice at least sound reassuring, 'stay nice and still..'

And then, she does panic. 'My little boy, I have to collect him at midday..' She's trying to look about.

'I can collect your little boy for you,' I soothe her, 'how old is he?'

'Two and a half,' she grins like she's just told a rude joke and remembered the punch-line. As I recall, I have to keep Charlotte talking and all she'll want to do is sleep.

'When did you meet, Chris?'

'We've been together ages..' Charlotte recalls, 'Four or five years..'

'That long?' I'm surprised.

'It's taken us ages to be a proper couple..' She explains, 'He kept waiting for his ex to turn up and spoil things..'

'I expect she would..' I smile mischievously.

'Oh she couldn't,' Charlotte smiles, 'I had to teach him to relax a little - after that things were great between us..' She recalls. 'That's why we have Scott..'; I'd like to say there's a twinkle in her eye: but I realise now it was probably her glitter make up streaming down her face.

***

The ambulance arrived moments later, by then Charlotte was getting edgy, looking for her shopping bag, and the lady in the brown coat had gone off to find some bandages, there was a worrying moment when Charlotte couldn't feel her legs: but I couldn't feel mine either, it was that sort of day.

I did find her wallet, fumbled through it hoping to catch a glance of her perfect little world - and this man named Chris who had bought such a smile to her face: life really wasn't fair was it? If I'd hoped to bundle her off in the ambulance and try and pretend today had never happened: fate and Charlotte were calling for me.

'You best go with her Miss,' the paramedic advised, after they'd made her comfortable.

'Of course I will..' I tried to smile back, Charlotte was delighted to see me, but soon drifted off under the strength of her painkillers.

159

***

'I can't thank you enough..' Charlotte's laying back in her hospital bed, "If you hadn't come along.." From way down the hall there's a carol playing, "Oh come all ye faithful" merges to the squeak of trolleys.

'It's okay,' I smile back, 'although, they say you're going to be sore for a while..'

'I'm lucky to be alive,' she nods, letting her head rest on the pillow. 'I never even saw what hit me,' she sighs, 'If you knew me you probably wouldn't think I was worth all your trouble ..'

'Oh why's that?' I frown.

'My Mother says I had Scott to trap Chris, that's why this has happened..' Charlotte grimaces, 'Fate's been waiting to get back at me.'

'That's nonsense!' I smile, looking into her bruised face 'Fate is a very good friend of mine and that's why it made sure you were alright..'

'I was scared,' Charlotte admits, 'That Chris would dump me, so I suppose I did trap him.' She looks at me sadly. 'And this Christmas was going to be so special for us..'

'Well,' I frown, 'I'm sure it will still be memorable..'

Charlotte agrees, resting her head on the pillow. 'Did you find Chris, so he could collect my little boy?'

'There's no need to worry,' I try to assure her, 'I've arranged for us all to meet up here..'

'How can I ever thank you?' She sighs.

'I just happened to be driving past, that's all..'

'-But you knew just what to do..'

'Oh that wasn't difficult.' I assure her, 'Terry persuaded me to take a first aid course..'

'-Terry?'

'My husband,' I hesitate, 'my soon to be ex-husband!'

'Oh I'm sorry,' Charlotte sighs, 'What happened?'

'Well, apparently he's replaced me with a younger model..' I

160

cough, 'I'm afraid it all gets a bit vulgar after that..'

'What a swine!' Charlotte blinks, 'If that happened to me, well there's no way it would happen: but I'd want to kill her, I mean there are children involved, right?'

'You could say that..' I nod.

'I don't know how you can stay so calm,' she hesitates, 'but then, you're a nice person: I'd want to rip her eyes out!'

'-And, what would that achieve?' I shake my head dejectedly, 'I mean she's already blind..'

Charlotte frowns back at me.

***

I'm strolling down the hallway just beyond the intensive care unit when we come face to face: I mean I've already seen him in her wallet; I needed to identify her you see - and locate Chris.

'Hello!' I step forward - and he's puzzled. 'Can I call you Chris?'

'What happened?' He's staring at me, 'They said they'd been this accident.'

'She's fine Chris..' He looks so relieved and yet so bewildered, he doesn't know how to react - then he just looks shocked. 'Your little boy's fine too!' I smile, 'Looks just like his dad.' I realise. 'She's going to be very sore for a while,' I reason, 'Tender, fragile,' I hesitate. 'She'll be wanting reassurance that you still find her attractive.' I shake my head, 'She's going to be wondering why me? What did I do to deserve this? And the thought of letting you touch her - or even thinking of you two making love will make her feel physically sick ..' I grimace, 'In fact I'm amazed just how alike we both are..'

'What did you do?' He grimaces.

'She was smiling so contentedly - then she just stepped right out in front of me!' I recall, 'I barely saw her.' I despair, 'But I couldn't just leave her lying there whoever she was..' I recall the moment. 'I think we both need to have our eyes checked. Because the last time I checked you were my husband!'

© 2006

161

When She's Returned to Me

I've just been looking at the chicken; there's too much of it - I thought, I hoped they'd be another guest at the table. I was wrong, it seems I'm always wrong where Justine's concerned; I shan't make that mistake again.

As I prise open the tin foil I want to toss the whole lot into the compost bin - and I'm just thinking about checking the answer-phone messages - when, I hear it.

There he stands, there's the gentle jar of the doorbell and, well sometimes you just know; you know? How sometimes you can feel someone's presence before they've arrived? Long before their arrival you hear the sounds, like in a distant dream - and you hear their footsteps scrunching on the path - and it has been snowing: but it's been snowy hazy and difficult everyday since, I last saw Justine...

And, as I open the door it's like I've already heard what he's going to say - only he doesn't speak - his eyes, they say it: and to be honest I'm not really listening anyway, not to him; I can hear the audio tape of her voice, it seems so long ago, in a distant Christmas.

'Mrs Stevens?' He nearly whispers it.

'Yes?' I edge forward, and I'm distracted, there's a milk bottle splintered on the doorstep, it was probably smashed in last nights gales - and that's really silly; some carol singer might come round and cut themselves on that - and then sue me for the privilege - and that would be really silly because Christmas is finishing today.

And, do you know what I'm wearing? "The twelve days of Christmas" apron that my sod of a daughter bought for me - and I really have to clean up that glass - where's the dustpan gone?

'Excuse me,' I'm backing away. I figured out long ago that I wouldn't find out the truth in one of her letters; her letters were all lies about how she was having a lovely time - lies.

Oh, I'm sorry he was going to speak; and you at least might be interested. Me? I want to shut the door, I want to walk away; I don't want to hear his truth.

'Mrs Stevens,' he's trying again.

'Yes?'

'-It's your daughter Mrs Stevens, Patricia,' he blinks. 'We think, we've found her.'

That's so selfish. Last time it was Christmas when she came back to us - and now, and now - Christmas is over; we're putting the tree back in it's box to hoist it back into the loft; cards are left dangling in the sitting room; the Radio Times is lost, the Christmas Telly Guide long since dissected.

A pile of Videotapes have formed a tower by the drinks cabinet - whoever said that video was dead - not to me, how could I part with those memories, Justine filmed them; those conversations are priceless; you can hear her speak, and she stays in the frame.

'Justine?' You can hear me calling: or you hear her on the old audio tapes; she's not following a script, she hasn't figured out what she's going to say; our Justine totally spontaneous - with no safety net...

'Mum, you mustn't worry about me because I'm fine, I'm eating well, I'm fine!' She croaks down the phone.

'Where are you?'

'That's not important, I got a Summer Job. Just had to get away..'

Last time, it was Christmas when she came back to me.

'Justine,' I smile; there's two years worth of presents for her: I never gave up hope you see, 'Only, I didn't know your size.'

'Mum..' She wants to say all this carefully worded response: and I don't even know if I should hug her.

'You never gave me a chance.' I shake my head to clean my tear ducts out, only it doesn't work. Then, I recall looking at her and, melting. 'Darling.' I wail back - and she's crying saying how it was difficult to talk to me - me? I haven't cut myself off for two years

'You'll never know how reasonable I could have been..' I stand strong peering into the chair at this miracle of a tiny baby girl; Becky, Becky is Justine in miniature - she's wearing the sweetest of pink dresses. 'So, she's your baby.' I bite my tongue, 'I'm not so unpleasant, am I?'

Justine doesn't reply, her daughter is walking towards me - how

163

dare my granddaughter be walking unaided.

'Was it fun?' I spit out.

'-Mother?'

'Keeping her from me?' I sigh, 'And where's her father? I'm curious.

'He's someone that was very special to me.' She recalls with a look that hides the complex dimensions of a far away love life.

'I'm sorry,' I touch at her arm, looking at her wrists, thinking, 'I'm sure that you wouldn't have slept with just anyone..'

'No,' Justine nods, 'I wouldn't have..' ; I nod, I know my daughter - at least I hope I do. And it wouldn't have been like that - of course this is all a dream, there never was a phone call; at least not one we got to hear about and little Becky dissolved that next Christmas, I awoke suddenly to study her picture in the frame in the bedroom; from Justine there was never a voice: until now..

You see, however she returned to us, it would have gone like this; telling others not to crowd her while smothering her in my own self pity, I'd of liked to think that at Christmas while I nuked the chicken, not the turkey because Christmas had been long since cancelled in this household: I'd like to think that she'd come back, not a letter or a garbled phone call - our Justine in the flesh.

The first year she'd gone, we'd visited London to look for her - what a waste of time that was! In the intervening five months she'd very definitely gone through puberty to avoid us - or so the ident man had speculated. Shortly after that we'd reasoned that Justine didn't want to be found...

'You think you've found her?' A doorstep is never colder than when you're waiting to go back inside. 'Only,' I frown, 'you can't be sure?'

'We can be very sure, Mrs Stevens.'

'She's contacted you?' I ask him, but he isn't saying he doesn't want to talk our business on the doorstep; he'll leave that for the Media frenzy that will no doubt dissect us over the coming few days - no doubt.

164

'You better come in,' I breathe, 'I'll put the kettle on,' I expect we're in for a long night. Christmas is over, the tree's in the box, drawing pins lay in a bewildered huddle on the coffee table - our Justine will be on the news tonight, and she'll probably never be more famous; and we'll appeal to the press and the public to let us recover from our ordeal and leave us in peace - and they'll dissect us on every opinion page and Tv Channel from here to John O Groats, watching every movement to bring closure to Justine's story; 'Closure' is such a cold and so American word. Meanwhile for now, Christmas is over - it's a wrap!

The Height of True Love

'Oh Mum, I can't believe I'm telling you, this - but I've met the most amazing Man! And it was so totally out of the blue: we didn't hit it off not at first, you know how you've never believed in love at first sight? Well nor do me and Stewart: but he was great, I can hardly believe it now; he saved my life, well it was bananas - really, he just turned up at that little green grocers where I did Saturday mornings.

"Do you like bananas?" He smiles at me with childish glee.

"I do.." I smile back.

He makes a joke about that being part of a wedding ceremony - and we better stop."Not that I wouldn't marry you," He says ogling the satsumas,"I think you're gorgeous, Sharon!" he just comes right out and says it - and I'm stunned.

"Thank you very much," well I must have been blushing by then, I go bright red like a blotchy tomato, because Mum as you know, that doesn't happen very often.

He peers at me, "'Sharon', that is your name, isn't it?"

"Yes.." I'm nodding patiently, "And, what's your name?"

"-Stewart,"

"I'm pleased to meet you Stewart," I smile back, offering him my hand which he starts to shake extremely enthusiastically.

"I bet you're wondering how I know your name," he's grinning at me - showing many misaligned teeth. "It's on your breast pocket.." He sniggers, covering his mouth, he then tells me where I can find his name tag: but I explain the occasion won't arise. "Oh, I said 'breast' Mum will be cross with me!"

"Well I won't tell her," I promise glancing at my watch.

"I think you're a very nice lady."

"Thank you.." I say, smiling at peering down at him quizzically. Stewart's always going to be a man who makes you ask more questions than he answers, and you know you taught me Mum to always see the good in people, just because they're different doesn't mean they can't feel loved? And I'm thinking just how lovely it was to have anyone's attention and just to feel special: so I return his compliment, "And I think you're a very nice.."

And, he's gone -I realise sadly, another customer barges in and I don't feel special any-more.

So it was a couple of weeks before I saw him again, and he's bought me flowers lupins I think, well my boss is in a mood so I put them in the tearoom where they dried out, withered and died: but that's another story I was getting to.

"Oh, how thoughtful!" I sniff them, I'm knocked back by their scent - and by Stewart's kindness: but I'm also very worried, when I ask people about Stewart, they draw a blank; I thought he was just a little boy with a crush, so you have to be cruel to be kind don't you mum? Nip these things in the bud to pardon the cliché.

I reach down to make eye contact. "-But you shouldn't spend all your money on me," I scold him, gently, "Won't your Mum be very cross?"

"I told her not to interfere!" He glares up at me, "I said I was in love with you and I was going to ask you out for a dance, tomorrow night. I love you Sharon!"

I know: but some people have strong feeling Mum even for me: so I'm staggered Mum because I didn't have those sort of feelings, I'd never experienced them for anyone - let alone someone possessive, like Stewart: so I did what you always said, be honest.

"Well I had no idea," I say gazing down on him, "I don't want to hurt your feelings: but couldn't you date someone a little like your own age?"

Well, he just stalks out and slams the door - and Stewart isn't the only one who's gutted, we both were.

Later that afternoon my boss calls me into his office: "Sharon," he says, "I'm finding this very hard to believe, but a customer has made a complaint against you. He says you were rude to him."

I mean how was I to know?

"Stewart says you told him to-"

"-Date someone more his own age," I glare, "Well it's true. He's become infatuated with me, so I let him down, I was gentle, I promise you.." I can feel that I'm struggling to hold on to my job here - so my boss explained, Stewart and I we're the same age: from what my Boss tells me, Stewart had some growth problems.

167

"So to you he might appear, younger or smaller - and he's also very shy and less experienced in areas we might take for granted.."

'Less experienced' Mum doesn't that make you laugh?

As you've always said I'm a tall girl, nearly six foot, with long legs so everyone is small to me - and that doesn't make it easy to date - and this small person had lain his heart on the line and I'd stomped on it in my ladylike way - but as you always quoted, true love, it does not run smooth, sometimes a girl's got to make the effort..

"Hello Stewart.." I sweat at the end of the phone line, "Please forgive me.." It's his Mum - fortunately she's quick to forgive and mediates between us, and we do have a lot in common, well apart from the fact that he's an outrageous flirt, who's not nearly as inexperienced as you might think, a real charmer as it turns out and a fantastic kisser; our date is amazing, opposites sometimes really do attract - and I guess I helped Stewart to overcome his shyness - because six months on we're still dating, not each other obviously; it was neck-ache that came between us, you see Stewart found love on that dance floor - and so did I thanks to Stewart who's bought me together with this amazing man, a chiropractor named Chris, we love to snuggle up together on Sundays with the newspapers - and he's since cured my neck problem I can spend hours in bed; and since I've met Chris that's what I love to do - and I can't believe I just put that in a letter to my own mother.

The Little Boy in the Mirror

I've been feeling very old today. I say to myself that we have days when we feel like this don't we?

My daughter doesn't like me using our electric blanket - she's been talking about the Eu - they don't like me to use it apparently: but it's the kitemark; it isn't up to current safety standards - of course not, it's too old - if they want me to stop using it let them come here and tell me, that's what I say.

I couldn't get comfortable last night, I was terribly fidgety: I tell her the cat's got fleas, he must have bitten me; she thinks it's "Restless legs syndrome," she's been reading about it from her posh encyclopaedia.

'Restless legs?' I say, 'It's cramp!' That's what it is, she says I'm probably right and goes to put on the kettle.

She's going to bring my grandson tomorrow, that's just what I need, little Keith - last time he was here he threw the worst tantrum - my word search somehow ended up in the rubbish bag with the recycling. I did have some luck though, I managed to fish the remote control out of the fish-bowl; so I was very proud of myself - and I'm happy to report to Mr high and mighty optician that my hand-eye co-ordination is excellent and amazing though it might be to my daughter, Debbie, at my age - yes, my eyes are still my own! She wanted me to get them zapped with a laser beam to cure my short-sightedness; I'm sorry to say I was a little sharp with her.

'Honestly!' I said, 'Do you think I'm Flash Gordon?' I meant that she thought I'd woken up in this new age and was frightened by the technology - then I remembered, that was Buck Rogers wasn't it? Well, still Buster Crabbe played them both - so what's the difference?

So later, well I visited the local café - and looked up the pros and cons of eye surgery on this website - and that left me undecided.

Debbie's a good girl. Last year, when I took her mother on holiday, Debbie came here every day just to feed the cat; I'd sorted out a feeding timer: but Debbie explained that she just wanted to check the place over - and it was a comfort to her mother. She's "undecided" as well, she thinks glasses are "sexy": I think that sometimes "undecided" is a great place to be, you never have to commit to anything just consider the advantages for the rest of time.

Debbie's Mum is convalescing at the moment - it's nothing serious, she was trying to do the Can-Can and landed on a waiter - I'm hoping to see her at the weekend. Maybe I'll ring her: but I found a number for that electric blankets manufacturer and they're based in Hong Kong; they were startled when I tried ringing them - and to be honest so was I when I suggested it - in all my travels I never learnt the Chinese for "electric blanket" perhaps we'll buy a new one out of Mum's compensation.

So, today I got up and I felt cold. There's thick ice all down the high street - and the doorbell jarred at nine, I thought it was the postman - but there's Debbie, and I wasn't expecting her this early you see - and she's not happy. I've been watching one of those Silent Witness dramas - so when she's calmed down about my blood pressure - and how I shouldn't be watching programmes like that, I smile very sweetly and explain myself.

'It's better to watch scary programmes during the day,' I say, 'but I am sorry little Keith caught a glimpse of it.' Although it hasn't affected him nearly as much as she says it has.

'He'll be traumatised,' Debbie glares at me as Keith bursts out laughing. 'I'm sorry dad!' She relaxes, 'It was a bit tricky getting here through the ice.' She pauses, 'I over-reacted!' She sighs.

'Just like your mother..' I say.

'Well, I am worried that you're watching gloomy dramas, I don't like thinking of you, here on your own. You should move in, with us..' She suggests bravely.

'-And enjoy a diet of Thunderbirds and Blue Peter, I imagine!' I shake my head vigorously, although I do thank her for keeping an eye on me. 'I like all sorts of programmes..' I point out, 'And I like walks to the café , and it's nice to have some time to do what I want.'

'Dad, there's a chance, Mum might not be like she was, when she gets back..'

'I know, and I'm scared like you, but we'll keep positive shall we?'

Debbie agrees, 'You are pretty incredible!' She smiles, 'But Keith's dad will be home now, would you like me to get Keith out of your hair?' She asks, 'He can be such a handful..'

'I won't hear of it!' I grumble. It's true that little boy, he throws my books on the carpet; he has no respect for grannies fridge magnets or ornaments - and I'm certain he's going to be trouble when he's older: but Keith and I you see, we have an understanding - through Keith I've learned the secret of eternal youth; you see - when I'm feeling 'old' I can look in that mirror - and yes, sometimes there's an old man staring back.

Well, today Keith was looking in that mirror when I was - and he was intrigued by his own little cheeky chops.

He's glancing further in, when he turns and frowns at me. 'Who's that?' He pauses, then smiles, 'You look funny!'

And I do. I look at the crease in my forehead, my tired eyes; I look a state I can tell you.

'What's he doing in there grandpa?' Keith wants to know - so I peer closer - and do you know, he looks much happier than I do; I suppose he has a different way of looking at things - and that makes me feel so much better; so sometimes, I'll look past that old man, and if I try I can see that cheeky little boy this energy he lends to me, with his eyes all bright - and filled with wonder.

Put it on the Tab

"Oh, Martin? Hello?"

Mary was on that phone again. She didn't talk much about her new 'friend' but Ann was certain he was interesting; they were always having meals together or going out bowling, and the mystery man had yet to pass the Jessica test: Ann was sure that her daughter would tell a mile away if this Martin was a fake; kids her age would tell if he was genuine or not. Anne couldn't help feeling responsible, the office girls had been teasing Mary that she'd left it too late to find 'Mr Right', a slight exaggeration at twenty eight: but they'd spurned her back to at least looking: and she'd gone out and found him.

All Anne, and her workmate Tina knew was that he worked in the local Supermarket, had it not been for the text messages and curious late afternoon phone calls, well they were thinking he didn't exist; that Mary had made him up; After all, the only people working at the nearby Supermarket, were spotty teenagers weren't they?

"Okay, I'll prove it!" Mary smiled so sweetly that she lost ten years."We'll go after work, you can meet him then," she folded her arms, 'then, you can apologise for being so suspicious."

Tina replied she'd believe it when she saw him: and let it pass around the office that tonight would be the night they got to meet Mary's 'Mr Wonderful'...

Mary breezed into the store with her two friends close behind her.

"How we gonna know when it's him?" Tina wondered frowning at Anne, "She could grab anyone off the shelf and say he's the one!"

Anne had more serious concerns. "Those Bananas don't look very healthy..." She'd promised her daughter a Banana Sunday with Ice Cream: but these were all bruised.

"I won't be a moment..."; Mary dashed towards a door marked 'PRIVATE'. The next moment, a sly balding man in his early fifties breezed through into the store.

"Ladies, I can't apologise enough," He paused. "I'll get our shelf filler to check out back..."

"Is, that him?" Anne gasped, a nice enough man she was sure, but not the adonis from the 'special afternoon' that Mary had bragged about, Anne was feeling sick; probably the cherryade she'd swigged in the afternoon break.

"That can't be him, can it?" Tina frowned. Mary wasn't giving much away. Soon, enough the fruit was restocked, by the Store Manager. Just what had Mary said to get such swift attention? They both wondered

"Not him," Mary grinned, seeing their faces. "The nice young man, who stocks the shelves. He's my toy-boy!"

"You're Joking!" Tina prodded the melons. Studying Mary's face, Tina wasn't sure.

But Mary was insistent. "That's why he's hiding out the back. He's shy."

Tina hissed to Anne that 'shy' wasn't the word she'd have used. She'd been here a few times and the 'boys' in the storeroom, weren't Mary's type, they were her type!

By now, Mary was in her element. The bread was squashed; could she possibly have some blackcurrant that wasn't dented?

Sure enough, a new box was located in the stores.   Tina's favourite mag wasn't in yet? So, Mary clicked her fingers and scowled at the woman on the lottery machine.

"Mrs Johnson, Mary?" The assistant broke out in a perfect smile. "Yes of course!"

Tina and Anne peered around the aisles, hoping to snatch a glimpse of the phantom shelf-filler, Tina taking a moment to tidy her light brown hair - as sure enough out he breezed, a real hunk, with finely cropped brown hair; blue eyes and a body to die for. Well, Tina thought so anyway: maybe she'd accidentally drop her phone number, all was fair in love and shopping. Tina was going to settle this.

"I bet you're feeling a bit queasy?" She asked Anne.

"Just a cough," Anne loosed the top button on her blouse.

"Let's ask him if he knows Mary?" Tina's eyes became scheming.

"He seems very busy!" Anne found she didn't want to know: a

173

phantom boyfriend fresh from 'The Chippendale's', Anne had been there: better to keep a game alive than grab the wrong bloke.

"Excuse me," Tina lunged forward to read the shelf-fillers' name-tag. "Paul, my friend here's feeling queasy..." Paul brought her a chair.

Anne coughed most realistically. "-And a glass of water?"

"-A Glass of water?" Tina groaned at her friend, "Why not have some brandy and a pack of crisps while you're at it?"; Anne's Shakespearian tragedy had encouraged the attentions of the shop's Manager, who supervised Paul's efforts: no way could Tina grill the shy young lad with his boss giving them special treatment.

Anne clasped the glass of water thankfully, now steady in her chair. "Excuse me," she whispered, addressing the young man directly. "Our friend, she says, you're her tomboy!"Adonis frowned back, confusedly.

"Toy-boy!" Tina spat out, passing another annoyed stare towards her colleague.

"Which one's your friend?" Paul gazed out at Mary and a smile crossed his lips as Tina pointed her out to him.

"Is it, true?" Tina scrunched the piece of paper containing her telephone number as she asked him. "That you, know Mary?"

"Well if, she said it, it must be true!" He yawned, beginning an exaggerated stretch. "Excuse me ladies. Mary didn't let me get much sleep last night." The two office colleagues passed shocked glances between them, as Paul sneaked off with a grin to check on the frozen peas.

***

"I don't believe he's your toy-boy!" Tina goaded Mary as she studied the Pavlova's

"Oh, you've seen him?" Mary could rest assured that at least he was here, that was useful to know.

"He's a, real-looker!" Tina hesitated, "I reckon it's the Manager you've been going out with, you can tell us. He'd be okay. For you..."

" I, tell you what!" Mary pushed the trolley on, "Why don't I prove it?"

"How will you do that?" Anne asked, watching as Tina tumbled into the cold storage box for the last box of fish fingers.

"Well," Mary smiled, "my young friend, Martin from the storeroom, he says, I can put it all on his tab."

Tina smirked, Martin? When she knew the guy in the store was called Paul; Mary's little rouse had almost worked: but Tina had won the office sweepstake, although she wasn't going to gloat, sad really. "So, Martin has an account here?" Tina frowned.

"That's right!" Mary put some peppermints on the top of the trolley as they reached the checkout. "Yes, and he pays me back, as a thank you, for being so nice to him!"

Anne didn't want to know: she was still price checking the cat food sachets.

"She reckons her toy-boy's going to pay for all her shopping." Tina gabbled excitedly.

"Her, toy-boy?" Anne paused. "She's having us on."

"Then, how come I can use his staff discount?" Mary cheered. Tina knew she'd watch Mary's transaction at the till was hawk-like eyes; she had twenty quid on this...

"Sod it, I forgot the Spaghetti!" Anne dashed back around the circuit: so much for Tina's 'witness'...

Finally, Mary lunged with the trolley to the checkout; it was like a supermarket sweep; all her meat; her vegetables and a week's supply of magazines? She'd surely squashed her mushrooms.

"1O8.5p, please..." The checkout lady rang up the amount, waiting patiently for Mary's credit card.

"Ah," Mary smiled sweetly. "Martin Johnson will pay it, can you put it on the tab?"

"-On his, tab?" The young lady frowned. "If you'd like to wait a moment..." She locked her till. She reappeared moments later, clutching a notebook. "That's fine!" She smiled falsely. "I just want to add that," She hesitated, "I could lose my job for this," she whispered, "but, I've got to know Martin very well: and I think how

175

you, use him like that, it disgusts me."

Tina and Anne couldn't help feeling embarrassed. Mary seemed suddenly shocked and Tina couldn't blame her: checkout girls weren't supposed to ambush customers, especially if, they were called 'Lindsay' and Tina would complain.

"Still," Lindsay looked into the depths of the till for a five pence. "It's none of my business, and I'm talking as his friend, not his colleague."

*

'Mary...'; Norman the Store Manager, caught up with them all after the briefest of delays to chat to Lindsay. Anne had noted Norman and the young operatives puzzled glances.

"The game's up!" Tina smirked, as they waited in there increasingly warm car."Open a window!"

Anne did so; she was just as keen to hear how Mary explained

away the staff discount, although Tina's money was on Norman as a possible boyfriend: they seemed to getting chatty.

Mary patted the last bag of her shopping and couldn't help looking up the store manager's nose.

"There we are, Mary..." The store manager paused. "Who's tab will this be going on?"

"Martin Johnson's," Mary smiled. She thought she'd managed to put the girls off the scent; she did know Martin, and he was shy about her: as any nephew would be, when visited by his aunt in a place of work. The toy-boy idea? It had been him feeding the messages to her mobile.

The rest had been true; the special treatment probably, just her bossy nature.

"Ah," Norman looked deeply embarrassed. "I'm afraid that's my mistake, you see Martin no longer works here..."

Mary was amazed she'd dropped him off earlier this morning, she'd asked his help with her little plan to stop her colleagues' from matchmaking.

"Very hush, hush," Norman tapped his nose. "He was interviewed this afternoon, for a position at Head Office, they liked his ideas

176

about, cutting back on staff perks."

"I've really appreciated all your help..." Mary smiled.

"Not at all, it seems Martin's left a present for you: I'm quite embarrassed by this, which is why I'm delivering it personally."

'A present?'Mary snatched the envelope excitedly - shopping vouchers, perhaps? Her heart sank, as she gazed into the white envelope. '-A, bill?' She turned her back furtively on her friends' car. 'Would a cheque, be okay?' She sighed.

AND FINALLY...

Notes:

I'm finishing with two tales that I wrote in my gap year – Easter Eggs was a victim of bad timing over the video choice, so will face changes in other markets, my year away has left me with plenty of tales to tell and some good ideas to polish; sometimes it's all about timing...

Eye of the Beholder

"Honestly!" I growl. "What sort of an airhead confuses aqua-marine with green?" I want to know. Silence. "Can I have your name?"

"It's Lilly, Lil Donaldson," She says, adding bravely. "-And I completed the order.."

"I see, " I take a deep breath.. "Well Mr New has changed his mind. He wants a white parasol."

"Oh," Lil is clearly thinking. "One of last year's designs?" She says at last.

"That's right, yes!" I chirp."-And can I just check that you have his telephone number?" She does – but I ask her to reel it off anyway – perfect. "Well young lady," I snap. "I'm glad that you've been able to sort this all out – at last!"

So, my son, Chris comes in and he's straight on the phone to Lil – and he's all smiles and teeth. and saying it will all be fine; I only had to mention some problems with the order, although he doesn't remember Lil even when I help him recall her large bottom. Lil's a bit late answering the call - she's been up a ladder collecting his parasol – of course, Chris doesn't know what she's talking about they are quite a pair those two ...

We arrive at the store with plenty of time to browse – fortunately, I've been trying for most of yesterday to get Chris to come in and check the status of his order and, well Lil is looking daggers at me.

"Mrs New," she smiles. "Good morning, would you like a cup of tea or coffee? You'd be most welcome.."

"No thank you," I try my best not to smile.

Lil helps Chris to put some items onto a trolley – I can see how he's trying to watch her from behind, it makes a change for him not to be led astray by a pretty face.

"Ah well I'm sorry for the mix up Mr New.."

"-Call me Chris, please..."

"Chris," she considers. "Well it's all booked. The green gazebo with green bench and the white parasol."

"-White parasol?" He frowns. "It's blue isn't it?"

"Aqua-marine.." I groan looking at my watch.

"Your Mother said white.." Lil is adamant. "I changed the order yesterday.."

"Oh, this is ridiculous!" I hiss."I rang her up yesterday and I said blue, honest I did!"

"I'm sure white will be fine.." Chris blushes. "It doesn't matter."

***

"I've asked Lil out for a coffee.." Chris announces suddenly on that Thursday – he almost sees my smile. "It's just a coffee," he repeats crossly. "Just to say a thank-you for all her hard work on our order. You almost had her in tears the other day. She phoned up convinced she was going mad."

"But don't you think it's too soon son?" I rub at my chin."You've only just had your heart broken, I mean why risk it all again?"

"Because I l-ike thinking about her." He grimaces, "She makes me happy, it's nothing serious.."He tries to convince me.

Engaged?" I don't know what to say – which is a first for me. "But you haven't even, well you haven't known her very long at all – and she's a rather large, personality.."

"We love each other." He gulps, "And we'd like you to be happy for us.."

"Of course I'm happy darling, only.." I hesitate, "I haven't really got to know her – I can't think of anyone more unsuited."

***

"Mrs New?" There's a strange young woman in my garden, and it takes me a while to recognise her. I mean her face is strained and she

180

isn't smiling.

"It's Lil.." She smiles, "I wondered if we could have a, chat.."

"If we must.." I snort, "Would you like a cup of tea?"

She nods – and so we take tea under our new gazebo.

"I know that you don't think that much of me," Lil sighs. "You've always tried to make things difficult.."

"Oh really?" I frown, "So, why are you marrying my Son?"

"Because," she hesitates. "He thinks it's the only way you'll approve of us – that's why I want a tru-." Lil breathes out. "We're going to be family now and I don't want to fight.."

"I know," I sigh,

I know exactly what Lil means – and so one day soon I'll tell her about this trip I once took with my son to order some garden furniture - and this delightful bubbly large young woman that we met – that my son barely glanced at in fact, he was downright rude; Lil is strong with manly hips she's not afraid of heights – and, she can do mental arithmetic – but Chris just couldn't see it and kept snubbing her.

So I put some obstacles in their way – I had to, I couldn't risk that Lil's inner-beauty might escape him.

"A truce," I smile, realising I'd taken it too far – Lil's lost some of that 'appetite for life' I so admire; she's become dangerously anaemic worrying about trying to impress me – and I hadn't expected that they'd marry just yet - before she'd learnt to value me as a friend as well as a future mother in law; Still, I needn't have worried about Lil's appetite for life – before the year was out she'd be eating enough for two.

Easter Eggs

"-Don't normally see you at these things Peter.." Alison breezed across the crunchy grass to her old friend's stall.

"Well Adam roped me into it.." Peter frowned.

Alison surveyed the stall a little sadly. "Oh your archive.." She recalled, it must be strange to have a son that didn't think that you were cool because you still had a video collection.

"Dirty Dancing," Alison wondered if Peter would recall who bought that for him - or why it was so important- it didn't matter if not, it had been a long time ago.

"I know," Peter grinned, "But Adam's right about the DVD's. They take up less space and they have some interesting extras-"

"Oh don't tell me you're a guy who hunts for Easter Eggs now..."

"Easter Eggs?" Peter frowned, "Oh the extras.." He nodded.

Alison smiled, you could find them in the menus if you searched the DVD and there were all these books on how to spot them. "An interesting thing to search for..and you listen to the commentaries?" Alison fiddled with the video casing and yanked it open, she was searching for a very special comment of her own - did Peter even remember it was their film, did she even care?I mean just the thought that he was getting rid of it.

"I haven't listened to a commentary since Joss Wheldon told me I had too much time on my hands.."

"Oh.."

He brushed her arm, "I do remember," he sighed. "The label kept sticking, so I took it off.."

Peter smiled, observing her crestfallen gaze. "-But I keep it in a special place.."

Ah, well of course he would; it wasn't like him to just forget - not really, not important stuff. Alison studied the other items on his stall - she could tell a lot about someone from

their fairground stall; novels, old novels Mills and Boon, biographies and videos - lots of videos.

"I wish my wedding video had a director's cut.."

"Oh?" Peter forced a smile.

"Yes.." A further inspection uncovered kiddies toys and revolting plates in yellow and green.

This all indicated a man that was moving on. "I wouldn't have thought Mills and Boon was your thing.."

"-My wife's.." Peter grimaced.

"I see.." Alison tried so hard not to stare as she felt the cold morning biting into her like a breeze of disappointment. He'd kept that quiet - those feelings were soon side-stepped by

the warm revelation that Peter had his own world now; and to think she'd always felt so guity about leaving, especially how things had turned out.

"So," Alison surveyed the fields, "Where is she?" Having a crafty look round the other stalls Alison supposed, "Do I get a chance to meet her?"

"No," Peter caught her eye all serious like. "No, you don't.."

"I, don't.." Alison felt a chill again.

"-That's why we have the stall.." He explained, "We've got to downsize." He paused. "After it happened, well it hit us for six." He adjusted one of the plates away from the sun. "They say Car Boot sales can be therapeutic.."

"Well they lied!" Alison recalled. "They're harsh! You pack all your life into boxes - set up your stall and someone comes along who wants the lot for fifty p."

"Oh," Peter smiled, "Adam set the prices: nothing less than a pound."

Alison couldn't help a broad smile. "Oh, he's your son alright!"

"Oh, no.." Peter gaped, "He's my nephew.."

"Oh," Alison's hand went to her mouth. She blushed. "So you and,"
"-Tina.."

"-Tina, didn't have.."

"-No, well we.. tried."

"Good," She hesitated. "I mean," She picked up her foot to remove it from her mouth. "I'm glad you were happy.."

"Yes, we were.." Peter sighed. "I couldn't interest you in some Women's magazines, could I?" Peter pulled out a box from under the table.

"Can't you recycle them?" Alison asked, scanning through them hungrily.

"I could ..but I thought someone might like to read them, there's quite a collection.."

"So, I.." She let her voice tail off - this was a time for honesty. "I've always found them a bit depressing." Alison admitted, "They're always about young widowers who've, well haven't they?" She raged.

183

"And real-life isn't.."

"-Well, is it?" She hesitated. "No, sometimes the girl just goes off with a thug - or only realises they've made a mistake when her new beau crawls off with one of the bridesmaids.."

"Did he?" Peter grimaced, "Well I didn't see that coming.."

"-Me, neither!" Alison sighed, "Well it's been lovely to chat.." She surveyed once more the wreckage of Pete's life sprawled across the stall, "I tell you what, I'll give you a pound for Dirty Dancing.."

"Ah, I'm afraid that's not for sale.."

"-It's not?" Alison frowned, why even open a stall if you weren't in it for profit - and why tempt her with it? Was there a DVD version and did it even have a commentary - and had Tina even existed at all? Maybe you shouldn't ask these questions..

"That was a mistake." Peter glared back at his nephew, "It has sentimental value.." He drummed the lid, "I thought that if I saw the right person, they might, like to have it.." He smiled,

"Would you like it?" Peter asked, "As, a, gift?"

Alison nodded. "Perhaps if you're not doing nothing, we could, you could come around my place and watch it together."

"Maybe, one-day." Peter placed the video into a paperbag and handed it firmly back to her with a smile.

"Thank-you?" Alison wasn't sure that was the right response - no money had changed hands: but that had all seemed so cold. As she walked off back to the path Alison felt funny. That had been a little odd - meeting Peter like that: but maybe you shouldn't try and relight old fires - it would be a shame if they couldn't keep in touch though.

But later when Alison studied her gift she found that Peter had left his own special surprise - a card containing his home phone number and E mail address.

"So, Peter," Alison smiled as she reached for her mobile. "Perhaps you do like Easter Eggs after all.."

© 2008

184

AFTERWORD

THIS ENDS MY FIRST COLLECTION OF SHORT STORIES AND I HOPE YOU ENJOYED THEM.. SOME, ARE LACKING IN STYLE OR THE TONE IS WRONG OR THEY'RE NOT SUFFICENTLY COMPLEX, AND SOME MAY NOT BE TO YOUR TASTE – THEY MIGHT BE TOO SEXY, THE 'VOICE' MIGHT NOT BE CLEAR ENOUGH - OR YOU MIGHT NOT LIKE THE WAY I WRITE.

I KNOW IT'S 2014 – A FAMOUS MAN ONCE SAID THAT IF YOU PUT THINGS OFF FOR A DAY THE NEXT THING YOU KNOW IT'S A HUNDRED YEARS LATER – AND PREPARING TO PUBLISH IS LIKE THAT.

IF YOU HAVE A COLLECTION OF STORIES THEN GIVE THEM AN AIRING. STORIES, EVEN BAD ONES DON'T LIKE BEING COOPED UP- AND YOU NEVER KNOW ,I MIGHT HAVE STARTED A TREND – I CERTAINLY HOPE SO, BECAUSE STORIES BELONG IN BOOKS...AMONG OTHER PLACES...

Mark R